DRAGONS OF DELTORA

DRAGON'S NEST

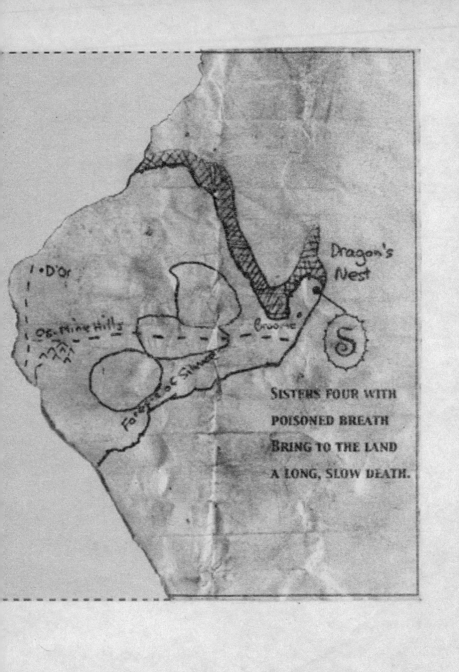

D'Or

Ol. Mine Hills

Forest of Silence

Broome

Dragon's Nest

S

SISTERS FOUR WITH
POISONED BREATH
BRING TO THE LAND
A LONG, SLOW DEATH.

A land of magic and monsters . . .

DELTORA SHADOWLANDS

#1 CAVERN OF THE FEAR
#2 THE ISLE OF ILLUSION
#3 THE SHADOWLANDS

DELTORA QUEST

#1 THE FORESTS OF SILENCE
#2 THE LAKE OF TEARS
#3 CITY OF THE RATS
#4 THE SHIFTING SANDS
#5 DREAD MOUNTAIN
#6 THE MAZE OF THE BEAST
#7 THE VALLEY OF THE LOST
#8 RETURN TO DEL

THE DELTORA BOOK OF MONSTERS

DRAGONS OF
DELTORA

DRAGON'S NEST

EMILY RODDA

SCHOLASTIC INC.

New York   Toronto   London   Auckland   Sydney
Mexico City   New Delhi   Hong Kong   Buenos Aires

For Reuben Jakeman

ISBN 0-439-81687-4

Text and graphics copyright © Emily Rodda, 2003.
Deltora Quest concept and characters copyright © Emily Rodda.
Deltora Quest is a registered trademark of Rin Pty Ltd.
Graphics by Kate Rowe.
Cover illustrations copyright © Scholastic Australia, 2003.
Cover illustrations by Marc McBride.
First published by Scholastic Australia Pty Limited.

All rights reserved. Published by Scholastic Inc., 557 Broadway, New York, NY 10012, by arrangement with Scholastic Press, an imprint of Scholastic Australia Pty Limited.

SCHOLASTIC and associated logos are trademarks and/or registered trademarks of Scholastic Inc.

12 11 10 9 8 7   5 6 7 8 9 10/0

Printed in the U.S.A.
First American continuity edition, September 2005

Contents

1 The Voice in the Crystal 1

2 Tales of Dragons 9

3 The Full Moon Meeting 19

4 Act of Faith 28

5 The Four Sisters 36

6 The Upstart 46

7 Dragon Hunt 57

8 Deadly Games 66

9 The Golden Eye 76

10 A Change of Plans 86

11 Signs of Trouble 95

12 End Wood 105

13 Sweet and Sour 113

14 A Message in Blood 123

15 Fears and Visions 132

16 Dragon's Nest 143

17 Fire and Water 153

18 Fight to the Death 162

19 The Sister of the East 171

1 - The Voice in the Crystal

Unwillingly, Lief joined the crowd flocking up the sweeping stairs to the palace of Del. His legs felt heavier with every step. The sweet morning air was cool, but his hands were slippery with sweat.

The other people on the stairs stood back respectfully to let him pass. Some bowed low. Many smiled and waved, thrilled to see their king among them. All whispered and pointed at the glittering jeweled Belt he wore — the magic Belt of Deltora.

Lief forced smiles and waves in return, but his heart sank as he saw how thin the people were, how shadowed were their eyes.

He looked up. The great carved doors of the palace yawned wide above him. Through the doorway he could see only darkness. And from the darkness . . .

I am waiting for you, little king.

The voice of the Shadow Lord struck, hissing, in his mind. He had been prepared for it but still he froze.

Are you greeting your miserable people, little king? the jeering voice whispered. *Fools! They look at you and think, King Lief and his brave companions Barda and Jasmine rid Deltora of the Shadow Lord's tyranny, and drove him back to the Shadowlands. King Lief rescued the prisoners the Enemy was keeping in slavery, and returned them to their homes. Now, surely, King Lief can make us live happily ever after . . .*

The voice trailed away in mocking laughter. Lief gritted his teeth and kept climbing.

He could not let the voice drive him away, back to the blacksmith's forge that was once again his home.

Tonight it would be a full moon, and that meant that today was the day of the monthly public meeting. People had come from far and wide to speak to their king. He could not disappoint them.

At the top of the stairs he looked back, as if to catch one last glimpse of the morning before the cold shadows of the palace closed around him.

A black bird was swooping down towards him from the pale blue sky. It was holding something in its claws.

Kree! Lief thought, his spirits lifting. *Kree, bringing me word from Jasmine! Perhaps Jasmine has decided to*

*leave Mother and Doom in the west, and return to Del
sooner than expected. Perhaps she is here now!*

Eagerly he looked towards the road. But he
could see no familiar black-haired figure among the
people streaming towards the palace. And as the bird
plunged downward he realized that it was not Kree at
all.

He stood motionless, watching it. The bird
wheeled above him, its yellow eye marking his posi-
tion. Then a tiny package dropped at his feet with a
muffled clang.

He picked up the package and raised his hand.
The bird gave a harsh cry and soared away, towards
the northwest.

The people on the stairs eyed the package nervously. Jasmine had begun training messenger birds
not long ago, so they were still an uncommon sight in
Del. And black birds had not always meant well in the
days of the Shadow Lord.

"It is just a message from Dread Mountain," Lief
called as casually as he could. He pulled off the package's outer covering and showed the note wrapped
tightly around an arrowhead and tied in place with
twine.

*You have stopped again, coward. Very wise. Now
turn and run, like the sniveling blacksmith's son you really
are.*

Lief moved quickly through the palace doors,
into the vast, echoing space of the entrance hall.

The hall was already crowded with chattering people. Lief knew that the noise must be great, but to him it seemed nothing more than a low drone. It was as though he were trapped inside a bubble.

Every sound outside the bubble was muffled. Only the evil whisper inside it seemed real.

Ah, you are closer to me now. Do you see your people before you, swarming like starving rats?

Lief looked down at the jeweled Belt. The ruby was pale. The emerald was dull. The gems felt danger. Evil . . .

"Lief! What news?"

The voice rang out, confident and strong, shattering the bubble, setting him free.

Lief looked up and saw Barda striding towards him, dressed for the meeting in his uniform of chief of the palace guards.

The pale blue uniform trimmed with gold was very different from the rough clothes Barda had worn when Lief had first met him. But Barda's brown, bearded face was the same, though his broad grin was a little forced. He looked at Lief closely as he clasped his hand.

Wordlessly Lief showed him the arrowhead.

Barda glanced around the crowded entrance hall, then jerked his head towards a roped-off hallway at one side. "We will get some peace in the new library," he murmured. "Old Josef is still at breakfast."

Lief nodded and together they stepped over the

rope barrier and hurried down the hallway. Soon they were standing in the huge, box-filled room that was Josef the librarian's despair.

Josef had not wanted to move the library down to the ground floor. The old library on the third floor of the palace had been his pride and joy. He wanted it to stay exactly as it had always been.

But Lief had insisted. The third floor of the palace was not safe. It had to be closed and never used again. For on the third floor, at the end of a sealed hallway, in the center of a bricked-up white room, was . . .

You will never be free of me, Lief of Deltora. Whenever I wish I can speak to you — and to others, when I am ready. Ah, I look forward to playing with those weaker, flabbier minds. They bend and break so easily. So easily . . .

Lief felt Barda's hand grip his shoulder.

"Do you hear him too?" Lief asked dully.

The crystal is the window through which my mind and voice can reach you. You will never be free of me. Never . . .

"Not as you do, I think," Barda said. "For me, there is only a feeling. A bad, bad feeling . . ."

Lief looked at his friend. Barda's face was grim.

"You should not be sleeping at the palace, Barda," he said. "This is getting worse."

"Far worse for you than for me," Barda said. "You should not have come."

"Even at the forge the whisperings enter my

dreams," Lief muttered. "And, in any case, the palace is the only place big enough for the monthly meeting."

"Then stop the meetings for a time," Barda said. "Until we can build — "

"No!" Lief broke in. "That is what he *wants*, Barda! He is trying to make me break faith with the people. Things are bad enough as it is. I should not be holding these meetings only in Del, leaving all the traveling to Mother and Doom. But I cannot take the Belt away, leave Del unprotected from that — that *thing* upstairs!"

Blindly he tore at the twine around the arrowhead and freed the note. As he smoothed the paper out, Barda gave a snort of disgust.

"Why does the old fool write in code?" Barda exploded. "We are supposed to be living in a time of peace!"

"The Dread Gnomes have always been suspicious folk," Lief said. "Perhaps the young ones will change in time, but old ones like Fa-Glin never will."

He shrugged. "And in any case, this code is as simple as can be — only intended to baffle the quick glances of strangers. See? Fa-Glin has just written out his message putting all the letters into groups of four, with no full stops."

Barda snatched the note, cursed under his breath because he had not seen the trick at once, then haltingly began to read the message aloud.

GREETINGS, LIEF, KING OF DELTORA!
THIS IS THE REPORT OF FA-GLIN
OF THE DREAD GNOMES.

IGRI	EVET	OTEL	LYOU	THAT
THEN	EWCR	OPEN	WHIC	HWEP
INNE	DOUR	HOPE	SHAS	BEEN
DISA	PPOI	NTIN	GTHE	VINE
SWER	ESIC	XLYF	REMS	HEFI
RSTA	NDON	LYSI	XBAS	KETS
OFSM	ALLS	OURF	RUIT	RESU
LTED	FROM	ALLO	URCA	RETH
EYAM	HARV	ESTW	ASAL	SOVE
RYBA	DMAN	YOPT	HEYA	MSHA
VING	ROTT	EDIN	THEG	ROUN
DHUN	TING	ISPO	ORTH	CREA
REFE	WFIS	HINT	HEST	REAM
IFON	LYWE	COUL	DEAT	THEF
RUIT	OFTH	EBOO	LONG	TREE
SLIK	EOUR	NEIG	HBOU	RSTH
EKIN	THEB	OOLO	NGTR	EEST
HRIN	ELIK	DTHE	WEED	STHE
YARE	BUTA	LLPA	RTSO	FTHE
MDIS	AGRE	EWIT	HUSI	TWIL
LBEA	NOTR	ERHA	RDWI	NTER
ONDR	EADM	OUNT	AINI	FEAR

YOUR RESPECTFUL SERVANT,

FA-GLIN

" 'I grieve to tell you that the new crop on which we pinned our hopes has been disappointing. The vines were sickly from the first, and only six baskets of small, sour fruit resulted from all our care. The yam harvest was also very bad, many of the yams having rotted in the ground. Hunting is poor. There are few fish in the stream.' "

He broke off, shook his head, then read on:

" 'If only we could eat the fruit of the boolong trees like our neighbors the Kin! The boolong trees thrive like the weeds they are, but all parts of them disagree with us. It will be another hard winter on Dread Mountain, I fear.' "

He handed the note back to Lief, his face very grave.

"So," he said. "More bad tidings. North, south, east, and west, it is the same story. But Fa-Glin did not ask for food to be sent, as the other tribes did."

"He is too proud for that," said Lief. "He would rather starve than ask for help. And perhaps he guesses that we have little to send, in any case."

Suddenly, he crumpled the note into a ball and threw it across the room.

"Oh, what are we to do?" he groaned. "The people have worked so hard, and we have given them every help we can. But it seems that nothing thrives in Deltora except weeds and thorns. It is as if the land is poisoned!"

"Or cursed," said a quavering voice behind him.

2 – Tales of Dragons

L ief and Barda spun around. Josef the librarian was standing there, leaning heavily on his stick. He had crept into the room so silently that they had not heard him.

"What foolishness are you talking, Josef?" snapped Barda, glancing at Lief's strained face in concern. "Crop failures are nothing new in Deltora. We were half-starved all through the years of the Shadow Lord's terror, but we hardly noticed it then. It is only after a battle, when you are safe, that you have time to fret about the sting of a small wound or the tightness of your boots."

Josef followed the big man's eyes to Lief's fixed, dread-filled expression. His face fell.

"Forgive me," he said, hobbling forward. "I am tired, and spoke hastily. Barda is quite right. The threat of famine has plagued Deltora for centuries."

"Yes," said Lief in a low voice. "But it was not always so, Josef. You and I both know it."

He pointed at the one tidy shelf in the great room — a shelf holding a row of tall, pale blue books.

"The early volumes of the *Deltora Annals* are full of tales of giant harvests, prizewinning melons, hauls of fish so heavy that the nets of the fishermen tore," he said. "When did things change? And why?"

Josef looked anxiously from his king's drawn face to Barda's, and back again.

"I . . . I do not know," he stammered. "It — just happened. Little by little. But I have sometimes thought . . ."

"Yes?" Lief leaned forward. "What, Josef?"

Josef wet his lips. "Only . . ." he quavered, "only that the land's decline seems to — to have followed the decline of Deltora's dragons."

Lief and Barda glanced at each other. In both their minds was a vision of the golden dragon they had seen in the Os-Mine Hills.

The dragon had been deep in an enchanted sleep, and they had not breathed a word of it to anyone, for its cavern guarded a secret underground world they had sworn never to reveal.

Barda cleared his throat. "I do not see how the land could have suffered from the dragons' extinction," he said roughly. "The beasts were a menace, by all reports."

10

Josef drew himself up. "I beg to disagree," he said. "Look! I will show you!"

He tottered to the shelf where the many volumes of the *Deltora Annals* were stored.

Barda clicked his tongue impatiently. "Oh, why did I give him an excuse to start messing around with those cursed books?" he said to Lief under his breath. "Now there will be no stopping the old bore."

"Josef," said Lief, "the meeting is about to begin. We really do not have time for — "

But the old man had already thrown aside his stick and seized a pale blue book from the shelf.

"I have always believed that the dragons of Deltora were linked to the land more closely than most people understood," he said, flipping eagerly through the book's yellowed pages. "Do you know, for example, that the dragons were divided into seven tribes, just as the original peoples of Deltora were?"

"No! Nor do I care," said Barda rudely.

"If you would prefer ignorance to knowledge, that is your affair," said Josef, turning from his book with a frown. "But the king, who has read my small work, *The Deltora Book of Monsters*, knows exactly what I am talking about. Is that not so, your majesty?"

"Oh — yes!" stammered Lief.

In fact, though he had glanced at the remarkable pictures in Josef's book, he had not yet found time to read the closely written words.

DELTORA DRAGON TERRITORIES

Dread Mountain

EMERALD

LAPIS LAZULI

AMETHYST

Tora

River or

Rithmere

OPA

Hira

Jaliad

DIAMOND

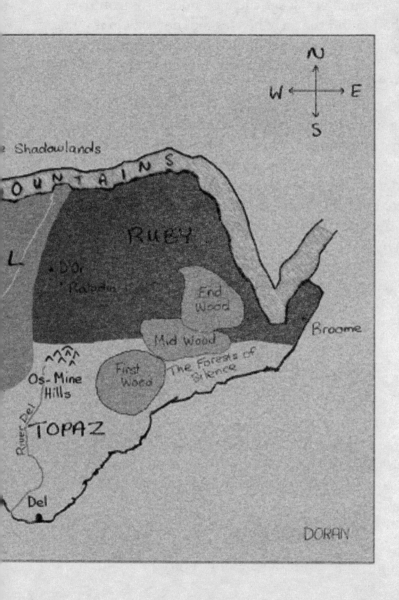

Fortunately, Josef did not notice his confusion. He had found the page he was looking for. On it was a map of Deltora — one Lief only vaguely remembered.

Curious despite himself, Lief moved to the old man's side and looked.

"This map was made by the explorer Doran the Dragonlover, long ago," said Josef, tapping the page with a bony finger. "Doran's maps were never elegant, but they were always accurate. This one shows the borders of the seven dragon territories. Doran drew it often, but sadly only one of the loose copies he made for travelers still survives. I keep it safely locked away."

"The borders look the same as the old borders of the seven tribes," said Barda, looking over his shoulder.

"They *are* the same!" exclaimed Josef excitedly. "That is just the point! The territories of the people, the dragons, and the gems of Deltora correspond exactly."

"And so?" Barda enquired in a bored voice.

"Do you not see how important this is?" exclaimed Josef. "You are not thinking, captain of the guards! Why, you of all people should understand!"

Barda remained silent. Josef looked at him severely.

"The magic Belt of Deltora, created by our first king, the blacksmith Adin, and worn by his heirs, protects the land from the Shadow Lord," he said in the

14

patient tone of one speaking to a very small child. "Each of its great gems — the topaz, the ruby, the opal, the lapis-lazuli, the emerald, the amethyst, and the diamond — came from deep within our earth, and each was the talisman of one Deltoran tribe."

"Barda knows this very well, Josef," said Lief gently. "Now, we really must — "

"Wait!" Josef commanded, stabbing at the writing beside the map. "Read what Doran says here. Read it!"

Once, the seven Dragon tribes encircled Deltora with their strength. The most ancient and wise of beasts, the Dragons were the guardians and protectors of their territories. Now I fear their time is ending. They are being attacked and killed in great numbers by the monstrous, vulture-like birds from the Shadowlands known as the seven Ak-Baba. Despite my pleas, the King does nothing, and the magic Belt remains locked away from him, in the tower.

The people are glad, because they can ill spare the beasts they lose to the Dragons. But I am certain that the Dragons' loss is

disastrous for Deltora, and was meant to be
so. They are being destroyed for a reason.
I am determined to search out the last of
them, and find a way of protecting them if
I can.

I leave on the morrow, and pray I will
not be too late.

Lief frowned. "Josef, Doran was a great explorer. But he was not called 'Dragonlover' for nothing. He was fascinated by dragons. He would have said anything to rally support to save them."

Josef sighed, and much of his excitement fell away, leaving him a frail old man again. "No doubt you are right," he said. He rubbed his chin with a hand that trembled slightly. Then he looked up.

"I am sorry to have wasted your time, your majesty," he said with dignity. "It is just that — I want so much to help you. Forgive me for saying so, but you are bearing great burdens for one so young."

Suddenly, Lief could pretend no longer. "I fear I am not bearing them very bravely at present, Josef," he said. His throat tightened and he bowed his head.

Timidly Josef put a hand on his arm. "I have lived long," he said. "I have lived through terrible times, and seen terrible things. But I have never lost faith. That is what saved me. You must have faith in yourself, your majesty, faith in your destiny."

"Destiny," Lief muttered.

"Yes!" The old man nodded violently. "You are the true heir of the great Adin, and not just because his blood runs in your veins. Surely it is no accident that you were born and raised not in this grand palace, but in Adin's old home? Why, day after day you worked with your father at the very same blacksmith's forge where Adin beat out the steel that was to become the Belt of Deltora!"

Lief gave a muffled exclamation, but Josef rushed on.

"You are heir to all the Belt's magic and power, my king," he said. "Surely it will aid you now. See how Del's topaz, the symbol of faith, shines for you?"

Lief's fingers slid down and touched the golden topaz in the Belt of Deltora. But still he did not raise his head or speak.

Josef glanced nervously at Barda, who was looking puzzled and almost afraid.

They both started when there was a timid knock. They turned to see the fluffy golden head and small face of Josef's assistant, Paff, peeping around the door.

"Forgive me, Josef, your majesty — oh! — and captain of the guards!" Paff gasped, her pink-tipped nose twitching nervously. "But — the people are growing restless. I was sent to ask you — "

"The full moon," Lief murmured. "Full moon . . . of course! But I need Doom. And Doom is in the west, in Tora. I must . . ."

Paff's eyes grew very wide. Her small mouth dropped open.

"Paff!" said Josef. "Leave us! His majesty is not — "

But Lief had raised his head. His eyes were clear and bright.

"Josef! A pen and paper, quickly, if you please!" he said. "Barda, I need the fastest messenger bird we have — Jasmine's favorite, Ebony, if she is here. And Paff, please let the people know that I will be with them in one moment. We will have our meeting and then — then I have something of great importance to tell them."

3 - The Full Moon Meeting

The meeting ran its usual course through the day. Reports and complaints were made, questions were asked and answered. None of the news was good, but Lief kept nothing back.

He knew that it was no use trying to give the people false comfort. They had eyes and ears. They knew only too well that times were hard. They would see through any pretense in a moment.

To be seen by all, he had to stand on the stairs that led to the upper floors of the palace. Just a little closer to the source of the voice that soon came back to torment him.

He fought it by keeping his hands on the Belt of Deltora — using the power of the gems, keeping his fingertips on the amethyst that soothed, the diamond for strength, the topaz that cleared the mind.

But the voice was relentless. Its poison dripped

into his mind hour after hour, till his stomach was churning and his clothes were damp with sweat.

Soon, he told himself. Soon . . .

The Belt cannot save you, little king.

Abruptly the voice left him. His head reeled with the sudden freedom. He became aware that Barda had taken his arm, that the people were staring up at him in fear. He realized that he must have staggered.

"I am sorry," he said. "I . . . am a little tired."

"The king must rest now," said Barda. "Thank you all — "

There was a stir from the crowd as a woman holding a sleeping baby scrambled quickly to her feet. The woman was gaunt, and her clothes, though carefully washed and pressed, were ragged. She looked nervous, but stood very straight, with her shoulders back.

"I am Iris of Del, bootmaker and mender, wife of Paulie and mother of Jack," she began, identifying herself as was the custom at these meetings. "I have a question."

As Lief met her determined eyes, he knew exactly what she was going to ask. Plainly Barda knew it too. The big man stiffened and began to raise his hand as if to say that it was too late, that no more questions could be answered.

"Yes, Iris," Lief said quickly.

The woman hesitated, biting her lip as though suddenly regretting her boldness. Then she looked down at the baby in her arms and seemed to gain confidence.

"There is something worrying my husband and me, sir," she said. "I am sure it must be worrying many others, too, but no one has yet spoken of it."

Lief saw that many people in the crowd were nodding and murmuring to one another. *So — the word has spread*, he thought. *All the better. It will make what I have to tell them easier, if they are prepared. I only wish . . .*

He opened his mouth to speak, then froze as there was a sudden stir near the doorway. Two women shrieked and ducked, a man shouted, and a small child gave a high-pitched cry of excitement.

Then the whole crowd was exclaiming, looking up.

A messenger bird had soared through the doorway and into the palace. Lief's heart gave a great leap as it sped towards him.

"Kree!" Barda muttered.

Kree landed on Lief's outstretched arm and waited until Lief had taken the scroll from his beak before squawking a greeting. Lief unrolled the note.

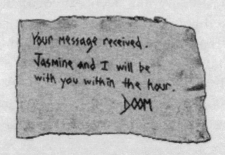

Your message received.
Jasmine and I will be
with you within the hour.
DOOM

"Thank you, Kree," he said, passing the note to Barda. He did not know how to feel. He needed Doom urgently, and was filled with relief at the thought that Toran magic was speeding him to Del. But he would rather Jasmine had remained in the west, in Tora, where she would be safe.

Then he shook his head. How could he have thought Jasmine would agree to that?

"I must have been mad," he said aloud. Barda nudged him, and he glanced up. Iris was still standing in the center of the crowd, looking bewildered.

"Go on, Iris," he said, smiling at her. "I am sorry for the interruption."

The woman swallowed, tightened her grip on her child, and spoke again.

"It sounds foolish, but Paulie and I half feared to come here today, sir," she said. "Especially as we had to bring our little Jack with us. We have heard rumors that somehow the Shadow Lord has returned — that he lurks here in the palace, in a locked room above stairs. Is that — could that be — true?"

"No, it is not!" barked Barda, before Lief could speak. "The Enemy has been exiled to the Shadow-lands, as well you know."

But Iris's anxious eyes had never left Lief's face.

"We have heard that the Enemy talks to you, sir, in your mind," she said in a low voice. "And perhaps to others, too, for all we know."

"That is so," Lief said quietly, ignoring the pressure of Barda's hand on his arm. "And it is time to tell you about it. I was going to do so today in any case, as soon as the time for questions was over. Thank you for giving me a way to begin."

Very flustered, not knowing whether to be pleased or afraid, Iris sank back down beside her husband. He put his arm around her and gently touched the baby's cheek with a work-stained finger.

The room was very still as Lief began to speak.

"On the third floor of the palace, in a sealed room, there is a thing called the crystal," he said. "It is a piece of thick glass set into a small table, and it has been in the room where it now stands for hundreds of years. The Shadow Lord can speak through it, as you or I might speak through an open window."

A murmur of dread rippled through the crowd.

"The Enemy once used it to talk to his palace spies," Lief went on. "Now he has begun to use it to taunt me, to distract me from my work, and, above all, to try to make me despair. He torments Barda and Jasmine too. And as he gains strength, I fear he will begin on others."

"But can this evil not be destroyed?" someone called from the back of the room. "If it is made of glass — "

"I have tried to destroy the crystal many times, without success," Lief answered.

His calm voice gave no hint of what those grim, exhausting struggles in the white room upstairs had cost him. But everyone could see it, everyone close enough to see the sheen of sweat on his brow, and the shadows that darkened his eyes at the memory.

He took a deep breath. The crystal was made by sorcery, and can only be destroyed by — by something just as powerful. The Belt of Deltora alone is not enough. But just before this meeting began, I suddenly saw another way. Tonight, I am going to try one last time to destroy this thing that threatens us all."

"Lief, what are you saying?" Barda muttered.

The murmur in the crowd had risen to a dull roar. Before him Lief saw a sea of frightened, exclaiming faces. The people were afraid. Afraid for him, and for themselves. They were right to be so, but panic would help no one.

"I cannot do this without your help," he called over the din. "Please hear me!"

Utter silence fell.

"These are the things you all must do," Lief said. "When you leave here, go directly to your homes. Bolt the doors, put up the shutters, and do not stir outside again until you hear the bells ring to tell you all is well. This is for your safety. Do you understand?"

The people nodded silently, awed by his seriousness.

Lief nodded. "Good," he said. "Now — there is

something else that can be done by those who want to help further. Make yourselves as comfortable as possible, and stay awake. Stay awake through the night and — as often as you can — think of me. Send me your strength."

"And is this all you ask of us, King Lief?" cried a man from the back of the crowd. "Our thoughts? Why, we would give you our lives!"

A great cheer rose up, echoing to the soaring roof of the great hall.

Lief felt a hot stinging at the back of his eyes. "Thank you," he managed to say. "I will carry your words with me. They will help me more than you can know."

✳

The sun had dipped below the horizon, and a huge full moon was rising, when six of Barda's strongest guards carried a shrouded burden from the sealed room on the third floor of the palace.

The guards were grim-faced. Each one of them was astounded at the enormous weight of the small thing they carried. Each was filled with a nameless dread.

Lief walked in front of the guards, Barda walked behind. Both of them were bent forward, as if in pain. But neither paused or uttered a word as they moved along the hallway, towards the stairs.

And because they did not falter, the guards did

not falter either. Suffering but uncomplaining, they heaved their hooded cargo forward, over the rubble of the bricks that had once blocked the hallway, past the old library, down the great stairway, across the deserted entrance hall, out of the palace.

Only when they had crossed the palace lawn and were moving down the hill did one of the guards speak. He was a guard called Nirrin, rescued not so long ago from slavery in the Shadowlands.

"Where are we going, sir?" he gasped. "It would help — I think — if we could know. Is it far?"

Lief turned to him. Later, Nirrin would tell his wife that never had he seen such a tortured face as when the king turned to him that full moon night. Only the heavens knew what the boy was going through, what was pouring into him from that nightmare beneath the cloth.

Nirrin had volunteered for this task, and never regretted it for a single moment, though he had bad dreams for months after that terrible journey.

He had heard nothing from the crystal, but still it had touched him. Long after he carried it, the weight of its evil seemed to press him down, to make it hard to breathe, even in his own safe bed.

And never would he forget Lief's eyes.

"The king just stared at me for a moment," he told his wife. "His eyes were like — like deep wells. His mouth opened, but no words came. It was as if he had forgotten how to speak. Then, he croaked out an answer.

" 'Not far,' he said. Then he pointed down the hill and across a bit, and I could see a sort of glow through the trees. 'Only to Adin's old home, and mine, Nirrin. Only to the forge.' "

4 – Act of Faith

Jasmine was waiting at the partly open forge gates, Kree motionless on her shoulder. Both were lit by a weird red glow, and shadows leaped behind them. Above, the great golden circle of the moon floated just clear of treetops that looked like black paper cutouts against the gray sky.

As the strange procession from the palace stumbled into view, Kree gave a harsh cry. It was plainly a signal, for it was answered by a shout from within the forge. The red glow brightened. Jasmine pushed the gates fully open.

Now the struggling guards could see the fiery blaze within, and the powerful figure of the blacksmith working the bellows, increasing the heat, the muscles of his bare arms gleaming with sweat.

"Jasmine! Stay — back," Lief gasped as the men behind him pressed forward, groaning under the weight of their terrible burden. But either he spoke too softly for Jasmine to hear or she chose not to listen. She darted towards him. In another moment her arm was around his waist, and she was half-supporting him as they moved through the gateway.

Feebly he tried to push her away.

"Don't, Lief," she snapped. "If Barda can stand against him, so can I!" Even as she spoke, the blood was draining from her face, but she held him tightly, and together they moved on.

They drew closer to the fire, and closer, till they could feel the burning heat on their faces. The blacksmith looked up as they approached. But still he worked the bellows, and the fire in the forge was like liquid flame.

"It is as hot as I can make it," he shouted over the roaring sound.

The faces of the guards changed as they recognized him, as they saw with awe that this man with the strip of rag bound round his brow, the blacksmith with sweat pouring from his black-streaked face, was the legendary Doom.

Doom. The strange name moved between them, whispering in the heated air. *Doom. It is Doom.*

Doom, the mysterious, scar-faced leader of the Resistance in the time of the Shadow Lord. Doom, the stern, solitary traveler. Doom, the ruthless one, who still held the ruffians of Deltora in the palm of his hand.

Doom, who had once sacrificed his whole world for his king.

And here he stands, Lief thought. *In the place where he belonged, before the Shadow Lord came, and everything changed. Where once he mended plows, forged swords, and made shoes for horses. Where my gentle, gallant father stood, too, in his time. And where, long ago, Adin made the Belt of Deltora.*

He stared at the glaring forge. Always before, it had been used to create. Now it was to be used to destroy. If he could find the strength.

You cannot defeat me . . .

He saw that the guards had begun to struggle. It was as if the thing they carried had suddenly become ten times heavier. They were dragging it now. Two were already on their knees.

You cannot defeat me . . .

Through a fiery haze Lief saw Barda push between the men and grasp their shrouded burden with his own hands. Veins stood out in his neck as he heaved, his teeth bared, the great muscles of his arms and shoulders bulging through his shirt.

The thing shifted a little. Barda heaved again. Closer to the flame, a little closer . . . close enough. But now . . .

They will never be able to lift it onto the forge, Lief thought suddenly.

Pain pierced his head, doubling him over, tearing him from Jasmine's grip.

Dimly he heard Doom and Barda shouting, Jasmine calling his name, but their voices were distant. The only voice that was strong and real hissed viciously in his mind, in the still center of a whirlwind of pain.

I am too strong for you. You cannot win.

Blindly, instinctively, Lief felt for the Belt of Deltora. His fingers found the topaz. The gem seemed to quiver at his touch. It seemed to melt into his fingertips, golden and warm. It seemed to become part of him.

Topaz, symbol of faith, he thought hazily. And into his clouded mind sprang an image of words on a printed page. Words he had suddenly remembered that morning in the library. Words from *The Belt of Deltora*, the small blue book that once he had carried like a talisman:

The topaz is a powerful gem, and its strength increases as the moon grows full. The topaz protects its wearer from the terrors of the night. It has the power to open doors into the spirit world. It strengthens and clears the mind . . .

The pain in Lief's brain began to ease. And as he slowly straightened and stood upright once more, it seemed to him that many others were crowding around him. Faces, clear and hazy, serious and serene. Shapes from the present and the past. Dozens of voices, hundreds, drowning out that other voice, speaking separately and together . . .

Have courage, my son. We are with you.

We will help you, boy. Have faith . . .

King Lief . . . we are thinking of you, as you asked.

We would give you our lives . . .

Lief bent and seized the shrouded thing that stood before the forge, and it was as if hundreds of invisible hands were beside his own. He looked up, caught a glimpse of the panting, exhausted guards, Barda's baffled face, and Jasmine's green eyes dark with fear.

"Stand back!" he shouted. And with one movement, he swung the evil thing up, up and slammed it upside down on the fiery forge.

Doom shouted in savage triumph. The guards groaned in amazement and terror.

The thick cloth covering burst into flames and disappeared in a cloud of ash. The wooden frame of the table, its stubby legs sticking upward, began to burn.

"Get it off!" shouted Doom. "The wood will choke the coals."

Jasmine sprang forward and pulled the table frame up and away from the sorcerer's glass it had supported for so long. She threw it aside, into the shadows, and it lay there, smoldering.

And then the crystal lay on the forge alone, revealed to all. It lay on the fiery coals, twisting like a live thing. Gray spirals edged with scarlet swirled on its rippling surface, and in its center was a hollow, whispering darkness.

Barda turned to his guards. "Get out!" he bawled. "Run! I order you!"

The guards scrambled up and did as they were bid. They were strong, brave men, every one, but afterwards none was ashamed to admit that he had taken to his heels and run for his life, the night the crystal burned on the forge in Del.

Only Lief, Barda, Doom, and Jasmine witnessed what happened next.

The crystal writhed, its center darkened. Then, with a hideous, grinding sound it cracked from corner to corner. Red sparks flew upward from the crystal's core, and a terrible howling filled the air.

Barda, Jasmine and Lief were thrown back, their hair flying around their faces as if blown by a fierce, hot wind. The bellows dropped from Doom's hands and he clapped his hands over his ears, his face a mask of agony.

But the fire of Adin's forge, where the Belt of Deltora had begun its life, burned on, relentless. The great topaz, which had summoned both the living and the dead to Lief's aid, gleamed golden as the full moon. And slowly, slowly, the howling died to a moaning hum, and the crystal began to cloud and soften.

Lief, Barda, and Jasmine crawled to their feet.

They saw that Doom had picked up the bellows and was moving back to his place by the forge. Doom's face was drawn but, gritting his teeth, he lifted the bellows and began raising the heat of the fire once more.

There was a sharp cracking noise. The humming abruptly changed to a low buzz that rose and fell as if hundreds of flies were trapped within the glass. Then, horribly, a thick, dull gray liquid began bubbling from the crack in the crystal, oozing across the glass surface.

Filled with disgust, Lief stumbled to where the huge hammer lay beside the forge. He picked it up, feeling its mighty weight. He took a sure grip on the familiar handle that had been polished to silken smoothness by so many hardworking hands. He turned . . .

"Come closer, Slave!"

The Shadow Lord's voice hissed from the crystal. Lief jumped, almost losing his footing as the weight of the hammer dragged him off-balance. He felt a split second of shock mingled with crushing disappointment. Then he heard the second voice.

"Yes, Master."

It was a thin, cold voice — faint, but clear. And it, too, had come from the crystal.

Lief heard Jasmine and Barda exclaiming behind him. He saw Doom's eyes widen in disgusted horror. The oozing liquid on the surface of the crystal was forming into the shape of a thin, cruel face. The shape's writhing lips moved.

"I am here, Master. What is your will?"

"Is the idiot boy Endon proclaimed king, Slave?"

"Yes, Master."

"And the Belt?"

One side of the gray face sliding on the glass bulged hideously, then shrank back into place. The thin lips curved into a smile. "The Belt has been returned to the tower. It awaits your pleasure."

"Ah . . . " The hissing voice sighed with evil satisfaction.

5 - The Four Sisters

A wave of fury swept over Lief, burning like the coals of the fire. He swung the hammer high and smashed it down with all his strength. The hammer head sank deep in the softened glass of the crystal, bending rather than breaking it. Gray ooze ran into the hot coals, sizzling, burning.

Lief wrenched the hammer free and prepared to strike again.

"No more, Lief," Doom said quietly. "Let the fire finish its work."

The buzzing was patchy now, coming in short, harsh bursts. Somewhere deep inside the glass, a feeble red light flickered.

"What was that other voice?" Jasmine shivered. "Why did it speak of Endon — of your father, Lief?"

Lief wet his lips. "It was a memory," he said. "It was my father's chief advisor, the spy Prandine, talking to the Shadow Lord just after Father became king."

"The crystal must somehow keep a record of everything that has passed through it," said Jasmine in wonder. "But now it is broken and dying, and it is spitting out snatches of talk meant to be locked up forever. Those buzzing sounds . . . I think they are voices."

"The sounds of centuries of plotting, betrayal, and wickedness, no doubt," said Barda grimly. "I have no wish to hear them."

He leaned over the slowly melting glass and spat on it, his face heavy with hatred. Then he moved to Doom's side.

"Your arms are tired," he said abruptly. "Give me the bellows. We need more heat."

Doom nodded, and Barda took his place beside the forge and began working the bellows steadily.

The glowing coals flared. The crystal began to lose its form and color. There was a faint clicking sound from deep within the clouded glass. Then the red light flickered dimly, and the voice of the Shadow Lord came again.

"The Four Sisters are in place, Slave. The Sisters of the north, south, east, and west. Have you done your part?"

"Oh, yes, Master. Everything you ordered." This voice was different from Prandine's. It was higher and more whining.

An earlier chief advisor to an earlier king or queen, Lief guessed. He felt ill, and began to turn away.

Then he heard something that turned his blood to ice.

"Good. The Sisters will do their work well. And the wretches of Deltora will never know what killed their land, even as they leave it, or die," hissed the voice of the Shadow Lord.

"But you will know, Master. And I," said the other speaker eagerly.

There was a long, low laugh. "You, Drumm? Oh, no. Like all good plans, this will take time to bear fruit. By then, I will have tired of your flattery, and you will be long dead."

Drumm whimpered, but wisely made no other protest.

"I have many plans, Drumm," the harsh, whispering voice went on. "Plans within plans, and all of them with one aim. Deltora must be mine. I need it for the gems and metals beneath its earth, and for its calm southern harbors, perfect for launching ships of war."

"I — I understand, Master," stammered Drumm. "And Deltora *will* be yours, as you wish. The Four Sisters will ensure that — "

"You understand nothing!" hissed the Shadow Lord. "If all goes well, Deltora will be mine without the Sisters' help. I would prefer to take the people alive. Even miserable wretches like them can work, and provide . . . entertainment."

Lief pressed his hand to his mouth to stifle a groan. He felt Jasmine grip his arm, heard Barda and Doom whispering curses. Straining every nerve, he bent towards the melting, collapsing crystal, shut his eyes, and listened.

Barda had let the bellows fall, but the coals still raged with heat, and the hissing voice of the Shadow Lord was growing more faint, more jerky and buzzing every moment.

"But if what that idiot soothsayer dared to say, before I tore out her tongue, is true," the evil whisper went on, "if there should come a time when a king rises from the people, like the accursed Adin, to wear the Belt and overthrow my plans . . . then, Slave, I will have the pleasure of knowing that this king defied me only to watch his land sicken and his people die. And I will have Deltora despite him."

"But —" There was a muffled sound, as if Drumm was clearing his throat nervously. "But, Master, if such a king should ever exist — which of course I hope he will not — perhaps he will hear of the Four Sisters, and try to find and destroy them. The enemy, the upstart whose name you have forbidden me to utter, dared to mark their places on a map, and — "

"That has been dealt with," his Master whispered. "The upstart has the fate he deserves. Also, the map has been removed, and my marks have been put upon it."

"But it was not destroyed!" wailed Drumm. "Surely it should have been — "

Too late he realized he had spoken too hastily. His next sound was a high-pitched scream of agony.

"Do not question my decisions," the voice of the Shadow Lord hissed. "Did you not tell me that you had followed my orders? That the part of the map you were given is safe?"

"Yes, Master, yes!" sobbed Drumm. "It is in a place where it could not be safer. Under my eye — and yours."

"Then this king will never find it. I dare him to try, and go more quickly to his death," sneered his master, and laughed.

The laughter was still echoing in Lief's ears when the glass of the crystal began to boil, and the red light, at last, went out.

✳

. . . *this king will never find it. I dare him to try, and go more quickly to his death.*

The ancient sneer burned in Lief's mind.

He knew that he was the king who had been foretold by the unfortunate soothsayer. He was the one for whom the Shadow Lord had laid a trap. He was the one who was destined to save his people from tyranny, only to watch them die.

It was long past midnight. The twisted lump of

melted glass that had once been the Enemy's crystal had been cooled, then smashed to powder and trodden underfoot. But the triumph the four companions in the forge should have felt had been snatched away from them.

They knew they should hurry to the palace, ring the bells to signal to the people that they were safe and the crystal had been destroyed. But none of them had the heart to do it.

They wandered into the forge yard and sat down together in the moonlight.

"It seems we keep solving one problem only to be faced with another," said Barda wearily, "It reminds me of those painted wooden birds travelers sometimes show — the ones that you can pull in half. Open one bird and there is a smaller one inside. Open the smaller bird, and you find one still smaller. And so on, until there is a bird no bigger than your thumbnail. And inside that is a tiny egg."

I have many plans. Plans within plans . . .

Lief stiffened. But the voice in his mind was only a memory.

The crystal is destroyed, he reminded himself. *That menace, at least, is gone. My mind is my own again.*

"The Four Sisters," muttered Doom. "Sisters of the north, south, east, and west. It is like a riddle!"

"The man they called enemy and upstart knew the answer, for he drew a map to show where the Sisters were," said Lief. "If only we could find out who he was! Our one clue is that he lived in the time of a chief advisor called Drumm. Josef can surely tell us when that was."

"The man himself is not important, Lief!" exclaimed Jasmine. "The important thing is his map! Drumm had part of it, hidden in a safe place. It may still exist."

"After hundreds of years?" jeered Doom.

"Why not?" Jasmine flashed back. "The palace is *full* of things that have been there for hundreds of years. That is one of the reasons it seems to me a tomb! And surely the palace is where Drumm would have hidden something valuable. He lived there."

"Yes. And he told the Shadow Lord that his part of the map was under his eye," Barda put in.

" 'Under my eye and yours,' " said Lief slowly. "That is what he said."

Suddenly, a startling idea came to him.

He jumped up. His heart had begun to beat very fast.

"And what was under the Shadow Lord's eye?" he exclaimed. "Under the Shadow Lord's eye, as well as Drumm's?"

"Is this another riddle?" growled Barda. "If so, I am in no mood for it."

But Lief was already running towards the forge. In moments he was back, dragging the blackened table frame that had supported the crystal.

"Under their eyes!" he panted. "What else can that mean, but this?"

"But it was in the fire!" cried Jasmine in horror. "If the map was fastened to it — "

Lief shook his head and threw the table frame onto the ground in the full glare of the moonlight.

"Drumm would have been more careful than that," he said. "If the map is in this frame, there must be a secret compartment somewhere."

He crouched and began running his fingers over the scorched wood. In moments Jasmine, Doom, and Barda had joined him.

The search was long. The varnish on the wood had swelled and bubbled in the fire, leaving the surface of the table frame so rough that Lief soon despaired of finding a secret compartment by touch, as he had hoped.

Then Jasmine cried out excitedly. As they all crowded to look, her finger traced a small rectangle on the inside of one of the table legs.

"A piece has been cut away here, then replaced," she said. "Do you see? The patch fits very tightly, but the grain of the wood does not quite match."

Lief, Barda, and Doom stared blankly at the table leg. They could see no change in the grain at all. But none of them doubted Jasmine. She had grown up in the Forests of Silence, and knew trees in all their forms as no one else did.

They watched as she fitted the point of her dagger into the edge of the patch only she could see. Soon a small block of wood had fallen to the ground, and Jasmine was slipping her fingers into the shallow hole now visible in the table leg.

"There is something in here," she whispered. "I — I have it!" Very carefully, she withdrew her fingers.

Between her fingertips was a folded scrap of yellowed paper.

"I cannot believe it," breathed Barda.

Gently, Jasmine unfolded the paper. It was a fragment of map, old and creased but strangely familiar.

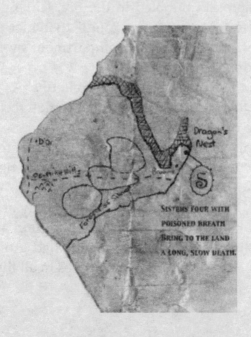

"It is Deltora's east," Lief breathed. He pointed to the large "S" marked on the map fragment. "And that, I imagine, shows where the first Sister lies."

"In a place called Dragon's Nest," said Barda. "I do not like the sound of that."

"It is the rhyme I do not like," said Doom.

And they all stared at the two lines of verse, which had been added to the map in a strange, bold hand.

Sisters four with poisoned breath
Bring to the land a long, slow death.

6 - The Upstart

When Lief, Barda, Jasmine, and Doom at last returned to the palace, they found it ablaze with light. The entrance hall was crowded with waiting people.

Guards and palace workers alike had crept out of their rooms and gathered together as soon as the crystal left the palace. All had stayed awake, to send strength to their king. The story told by the six guards who had run from the forge had only made them more determined to continue their watch.

Lief's heart twisted with pain as he saw the gladness on their faces, heard their shouts of triumph and relief as he told them that the crystal was no more. The yellowed scrap of paper tucked away inside his jacket seemed to burn him. The words of the evil rhyme tormented him.

As the bells began to ring and celebrations began, he slipped away to the new library. It was shadowy and seemed deserted, but a light glowed at the end of the room, from Josef's private chamber.

The old librarian was sitting at his worktable, with his back to the open door.

The table was cluttered with paints and brushes, and a half-completed illustration for a new book lay at Josef's hand. But the brushes were clean, and the jars of paint sealed.

Plainly, Josef had not been working, but had been sitting at the table out of habit. He, too, had been keeping watch.

Lief knocked gently on the edge of the door. Josef turned stiffly in his chair, frowning slightly. When he saw who his visitor was, however, his face broke into a radiant smile.

"Your majesty!" he cried, struggling to his feet. "I thought it was Paff. How wonderful to see you safe! I knew you would succeed!"

"It was thanks to you that I dared to try," Lief answered.

He moved into the room and took the old man's outstretched hands, shaking them warmly. Then he hesitated, not quite knowing how to go on.

"Josef, there is something I need to — " he began.

"I know," Josef broke in. "Ever since I first heard

the bells I have been thinking about it. And — you will be surprised — I have decided that we should stay where we are."

He saw Lief's confusion and looked surprised. "Did you not mean to ask me about the library, your majesty?" he asked. "About moving it back to the third floor, now that the menace has been removed?"

"Oh, yes, that, too, Josef, of course," said Lief hastily and quite untruthfully.

"It has taken a very long time to move all the books downstairs," Josef said. "I cannot bear the thought of carrying them all back again. Paff tries her best, I daresay, but I fear she will never be half the assistant Ranesh was. And she *chatters* so!"

Lief smiled, despite his impatience. Paff annoyed him, too, though at the same time he felt rather sorry for her. Josef was not much of a companion for a young girl.

But when Ranesh, Josef's foster son, had left Del and gone to the west to marry his true love, Marilen, Paff had timidly come forward and asked if she could replace him.

Josef had been pleased enough to have her. Paff could read and write, which was sadly uncommon among the young people who had grown up under the rule of the Shadow Lord. And there had been no other applicants for the job.

No wonder, thought Lief. Everyone knew that Josef was a fussy and demanding employer. But Paff, a released prisoner from the Shadowlands and the only surviving member of her family, had been anxious to find work as quickly as possible.

"At least Paff is hardworking, Josef," Lief said soothingly. "And we could give you other help to move again. Are you sure about staying here? I know how much you miss the old library."

Josef shrugged and grimaced. "I have complained very much, I know," he said. "I am too set in my ways. The fact is, your majesty, in the past weeks I have realized how isolated we were on the third floor. Here, we are in the thick of things. I think that the library will have many more visitors if it is placed where everyone can see it."

"That is certainly true," said Lief heartily. "Well, then, that is settled. Now . . . Josef, can you help me with some — some research I have to do, about Deltora's past?"

"Why certainly!" beamed Josef, rubbing his hands delightedly. "How can I be of service?"

"First, I need to find out when a chief advisor called Drumm lived," Lief said. "Do you know of him?"

Josef frowned. "I know the name. I just cannot recall where I have seen it," he muttered in annoyance. "But I will soon find it in the *Annals*, your majesty, never fear."

He began shuffling rapidly to the door.

Lief caught his arm. "Not now, Josef. It is late,

and we must both get some sleep. In the morning, perhaps. But here is something else to think about. Have you ever heard the phrase 'The Four Sisters'?"

"Ah!" Josef's face brightened. "Why, of course! *The Four Sisters* is an old Jalis legend — one of the Tenna Birdsong tales. It is about four sisters who loved to sing together. They sang so sweetly that they annoyed a wicked sorcerer, who banished them to the four corners of the land. But still they sang to one another, though they were far apart."

Lief nodded gloomily. *No doubt the Shadow Lord thought it amusing to name his sources of poison after four sweet sisters in an old Deltoran folk story,* he thought. *But this does not take me much further.*

"Yes, *The Four Sisters.* A charming little story, as I recall," Josef chattered on eagerly. "I have not read it for years, but planned to do so very soon, to see if it is worthy of inclusion in *Tales of Deltora* — my new book, you know. I will look it up for you now!"

This time he would not be stopped. He hurried out of his room and, with Lief following reluctantly, hastened to the shelf where the *Deltora Annals* stood.

Pulling the first thick volume from the shelf, he began leafing through it.

Suddenly, Lief could not bear it. He was bone weary, and even to please Josef he knew he could not stand and read an old folktale now.

Firmly he put his hand on the old man's, to stop the restless flipping of pages.

"Not now, Josef, please," he said. "I will look at the story in the — His voice broke off as, suddenly, his stomach seemed to turn over.

He was aware of Josef looking at him in puzzlement, but for a moment he could not speak. He stared down at the closely printed page on which his and Josef's hands rested. Was it a coincidence? Could it be . . . ?

"What is it, your majesty?" Josef asked nervously.

Slowly Lief straightened. He slipped his hand into his inside jacket pocket, and brought out the torn part of the map.

"Josef," he said, trying to control the excitement in his voice. "Before I show you this, you must promise me that you will speak of it to no one."

Josef bit his lip. "I know I have let my tongue run away with me in the past, your majesty," he mumbled. "But I have learned my lesson, I swear it. Any secret you share with me now, I will take to my grave."

"I hope it will not come to that," said Lief lightly. And, still wondering if he was doing the right thing, he unfolded the map.

Josef's eyes widened. "Why, how did you come by this!" he exclaimed in excitement.

"You recognize this paper?" Lief asked quietly.

"Of course!" Josef cried, touching the map with reverent fingers. "Doran the Dragonlover's mapping style is unmistakable! Ah, but what a tragedy that only a fragment remains."

Lief stared at him in astonishment. This was not what he had been expecting the old man to say. But . . . Doran the Dragonlover! Of course!

That was why the markings on the fragment of map — all but the verse — had looked familiar. They were almost exactly like those on the map of Dragon Territories Josef had shown him just before the meeting.

"What a fool I was not to have seen it," he murmured.

But Josef was not listening. His eyes had moved to the verse printed at the bottom of the paper.

"Not only has it been torn, but someone has dared to scrawl their own words here!" he said furiously. "What is this drivel? *'Sisters four with poisoned breath, Bring to the land a long, slow —'* "

He stopped, his mouth gaping. He swallowed hard.

"Four sisters," he whispered. "The Four Sisters . . . Doran . . . Oh, how could I have forgotten? Why did I not think of it! How could I — "

Frantically he pulled the fifth volume of the *Deltora Annals* from the shelf. He flipped through the pages until he came to the Dragon Territories map. Then he slowed, and began turning the pages more carefully.

"Josef, what are you looking for?" demanded Lief in a fever of impatience.

But still the old librarian did not answer. He was muttering to himself, completely wrapped up in his own thoughts.

"Now, where is it?" he said, glancing rapidly at every page. "It cannot be far now. Not far now . . . Aha!"

Recklessly he pressed the book wide open and pointed triumphantly at the left-hand page, which was covered with Doran's writing.

"Here it is!" he said. "Doran's final entry in the *Annals*. Read it!"

"Josef, what—?" Lief began.

"Read it!" roared Josef, his eyes wild. "Read all of it! You will see!"

This is the explorer Doran, writing in haste. I returned yesterday from my journey to seek the remaining dragons. In grief, I tell you that not one still flies Deltoran skies.

And there is even more dreadful news.

I now know why the Enemy wanted the Dragons destroyed. He had a plan that the Dragons would not have tolerated.

The four sisters. In the far-flung corners of the land I heard whispers of them. If what I have heard is true, the sisters of the north and east are already in place.

The south, and the west, will surely be next, and I can guess where, if the rumours of the locations of the others are to be believed.

Whoever reads my words, show them to the King if you can. The King, wearing the Belt of Deltora, is Deltora's only salvation now. No-one will listen to me. They think I am mad. I hurried to Del without pausing to eat, wash or sleep. To these palace fools, with their soft hands and painted faces, I look like a wildman.

I must set out once more, to seek proof of what I say. Another long journey... perhaps my last, for I fear the Enemy is aware of me.

If I do not return, seek me where the Four Sisters lurk...

That was all. On the opposite page there was only a beautifully neat report of a palace dinner, written by one of the librarians. Heading the list of people who attended was the name of Drumm, the king's chief advisor.

Lief felt sick.

"Doran's words are wild, I know," said Josef softly. "It was said that his last, hopeless dragon hunt had sent him mad with grief. There are many references to it, later in the *Annals*. The thought of it always grieved Ranesh and me very much. Doran was a great man."

"Indeed he was," said Lief, looking down at the hastily written words. His stomach was churning as he imagined the desperation of the man who had written them. "And he was not mad, Josef. Unless being the only one to see the truth is a kind of madness."

He pressed the book even further open and pointed to a few tiny, jagged rags of paper clinging to the binding.

"Look," he said softly.

Josef squinted shortsightedly, then recoiled.

"But — but it looks as if a page has been torn out here!" he exclaimed. "That is impossible! Once a thing was written into the *Annals*, it was written! It was strictly forbidden for anything to be removed."

"Drumm would not have cared what was *forbidden*," said Lief. "He was following the Shadow Lord's orders. I think this is part of the missing page."

He put the fragment of Doran's map on top of the open book. It was clear at once that the thick, yellowed paper of the map was the same as the paper used in the *Annals*.

Josef stared, aghast. "Doran drew a map on the page opposite his words, to show where he thought the four sisters lurked," he breathed. "And that page was torn out! No doubt very soon after he wrote it, too, because the back of the map is blank. But how did you know?"

"I only suspected," Lief said. "When you were looking for the story of the Four Sisters, I realized that the paper of the map was the same as the paper always used in the *Annals*. It could have been chance — but it was not."

Again he stared at the final lines of Doran's message.

. . . the Enemy is aware of me . . .

He swallowed. "You said that this was Doran's last entry in the *Deltora Annals*?"

"Oh, yes," said Josef unhappily. "He set out to find the Four Sisters of whom he speaks. But he never returned, and no one knew where to look for him. He was never seen again."

7 – Dragon Hunt

A few days later, Lief, Barda, and Jasmine set out from Del on horseback, accompanied by a troop of palace guards. Lief carried with him both the fragment found in the table frame and Josef's precious copy of Doran's Dragon Territories map.

As far as the people of the city knew, their king and his companions were going on their long-delayed tour of the kingdom, beginning in Broome, far to the east.

Only Doom and Josef knew their real purpose. To find the Sister of the East at Dragon's Nest, to destroy it if they could, and perhaps, through knowledge of it, to guess at the hiding places of the other three Sisters.

"I would give much to be going with you,"

Doom said as he farewelled them at the city gates. "But someone must stay to deal with things here."

His mouth twisted in the familiar mocking smile.

"And in any case, the three of you have done well enough without me in the past," he added. "I might spoil your luck."

"I doubt it," said Lief, clasping his hand warmly. He knew what it cost Doom to jest at this moment.

They were now all convinced that the kingdom's future hung on this perilous quest. Hundreds of last-minute words of advice and warning must have been trembling on Doom's tongue. But he held them back.

He knew that nothing he could say could help Lief, Barda, and Jasmine now. He could only offer them his trust.

At a shout from Barda, the guards moved off, their heavy gray horses breaking into a steady trot.

With Kree swooping above them, the three companions followed. Their lighter, faster mounts, carefully chosen by Barda, snorted with pleasure, puffing mist into the crisp dawn air.

Lief rode Honey, a spirited golden mare with a flowing white tail and mane. Barda rode his favorite, a strong, sweet-tempered chestnut called Bella. Jasmine's horse was the coal-black Swift.

Lief looked back, lifted his arm to return Doom's wave, and felt a pang of guilt.

"Cheer up. What Doom does not know will not hurt him," said Jasmine's voice beside him.

Jasmine was grinning, relishing her freedom from the city. Her long black hair was already tangling in the breeze. Filli peeped out from under her jacket. His tiny paws were clutching her collar tightly, and his black eyes were very wide. Plainly, he found horse-riding very alarming.

"I am leading you into danger," Lief muttered. "And you are Doom's child."

"Quite!" Jasmine snapped, her grin disappearing. "Like father, like daughter. Have you ever known Doom to tell all his secrets? Or to shrink from peril, for any reason?"

Lief said nothing. The relationship between Jasmine and her father, that strange mixture of love, respect, and rivalry, was something he would never understand.

"Besides," Jasmine said, in a milder tone, "Doom thinks we are going directly to Dragon's Nest. There we will be facing the Shadow Lord's evil. Nothing we could do on the way could be more dangerous than that."

Lief was not so sure. He fought back a shudder as he remembered . . .

Barda rode up on his left. "As soon as we are well out of sight of Del, I will give the order to turn north," he said in a low voice. "If you are still determined to do this, Lief."

Lief moistened his lips. "I am," he said. "I feel it is the only thing that might help us. We need a weapon the Shadow Lord did not plan for. Powerful as the Belt of Deltora is, it may not be enough."

"Very well," Barda said grimly. "North it is. To the Os-Mine Hills. And the dragon."

✳

A day and a half later, they left their horses and the confused, nervous guards in a grassy space sheltered by the first rocky slopes of the Os-Mine Hills. Barda had put his men under the orders of Brid, his second in command, telling them that he, Lief, and Jasmine wished to walk into the Hills alone, to gather healing herbs.

"Did you have to tell that story?" hissed Jasmine as the three companions tramped away, the guards staring after them. "Herbs! Now Brid and the others will think this trip to the Os-Mine Hills is my fault! Already most of them believe I am a witch because I speak to birds and trees. Now, no doubt, they think I need rare ingredients for my spells."

Barda shrugged. "All the better," he said. "The important thing is that they do not suspect our real reason for being here."

"Why can't we just tell them the truth?" Jasmine exclaimed. "They will find out soon enough, if we come back to them leading a golden dragon!"

"*Leading* it?" growled Barda. "It is more likely that we will be running from it in terror."

"We have to keep the entrance to the underground world secret, Jasmine, you know that!" said Lief. "And, in any case, the guards would panic if they knew what we planned. Dragons have an evil reputation. If the topaz dragon *does* rise, and *does* agree to help us fight the Sister of the East, it must seem a complete surprise."

"It *will* be a great surprise, as far as I am concerned, if the dragon does anything but try to eat us," Barda snorted. "That is, if it wakes at all."

"It will wake," said Lief, with a confidence he did not feel. "The presence of the Belt of Deltora in its territory will make it stir. I am sure of it."

"I am hoping that the Belt will also protect us from our old friends the Granous," Barda said. "It has killed evil creatures before, at the height of its power."

Lief remembered the sharp yellow teeth and stinking breath of the bloodthirsty, game-playing creatures that hunted in packs over these hills.

He did not relish the idea of becoming a prisoner of the Granous again. But he knew he could not depend on the Belt to save him.

"The Granous are wicked, but they are not creatures of the Shadow Lord," he said in a low voice. "They are of Deltora. The Belt may weaken them, but that is all, I fear."

They had walked for an hour. The sun was high in the sky when Jasmine stopped abruptly, lifted her head, and seemed to listen.

"What is it?" Lief whispered.

Jasmine murmured to Kree, and the black bird took flight. He wheeled overhead, and in moments was back on Jasmine's shoulder, squawking rapidly.

"Granous," Jasmine said briefly. "In a clearing not far over the next rise."

"We must find a way around them," said Barda. "We cannot afford a fight now. Tell Kree — "

He and Lief froze as suddenly a wail of terror echoed through the hills.

"If we are careful, the creatures will not hear us, or smell us either," Jasmine said calmly. "They are well occupied. They already have a prisoner."

Her companions stared at her in dismay.

She met their eyes coolly. "It is good fortune for us," she said. "We would be well advised not to interfere."

"But we cannot knowingly leave someone at the mercy of the Granous!" Lief hissed. "They will ask him their infernal riddles, and when he cannot answer them they will start biting off his fingers and toes. They will kill him, Jasmine!"

"Better that they kill a stranger than that they kill us," Jasmine said. And Lief knew that she was repeating a lesson she had learned only too well in the terror that was the Forests of Silence.

For a moment he hesitated. He knew that he should not let his heart rule his head in this. But then the piteous cry came again, followed by a scream of pure agony.

"No!" Lief breathed. He started forward.

"Wait! I will go back and fetch the guards," said Barda, catching at his arm.

Lief pulled himself free. "There is no time for that!" he muttered. "Come with me or not, as you like."

He began to run, and Jasmine and Barda followed, as he knew they would.

Panting, the three scrambled up the next hill. When they reached the top they flattened themselves on the ground and crawled forward until they could see the ground below.

The other side of the hill fell away into a treacherous, pebbly slope ending in a tumble of parched rocks. Beyond that was a grove of stunted trees, from which came the faint sounds of moaning and sobbing mingled with rough laughter.

They began picking their way down the slope. Their progress was agonizingly slow. The sounds from the trees were growing louder and more disturbing.

Lief's heart was pounding. He was sickened by the thought of what was happening in the grove. As soon as he reached level ground and the trees were straight ahead, he reached for his sword.

"Do not even *think* of charging in there, Lief!"

Barda whispered fiercely in his ear. "We will have no chance in hand-to-hand combat with twelve Granous! We must try to separate them."

Lief gritted his teeth and nodded. Desperate as he was to free the sobbing, groaning man within the grove, he knew that Barda was right.

"Jasmine, you come with me," Barda ordered. "We will try to lure some of them away. Lief, there is probably a clearing in the center of the grove. Move around it and get behind the prisoner. Cut his bonds if you can, but keep out of sight until I give the signal."

They separated. Lief crept around the trees until, through a gap, he saw movement. He moved in a little, and his stomach turned over as he suddenly gained a clear view of what was happening in the clearing.

The Granous were gathered around someone who was sitting at the clearing's edge. Their shaggy gray bodies almost hid their victim. Lief could only see a mop of curly brown hair, hunched shoulders shrouded in a brown cloak, and a hand clutching another hand, from which bright red blood streamed.

"Time for the next question!" the biggest of the Granous cackled. "Another question, another finger!"

The others danced backwards, screaming with pleasure and snapping their jaws. Then Lief saw the sobbing victim clearly for the first time.

He was sitting propped against a tree, bound in place by strong vines. From the waist up, he looked like a man. But from the waist down he was covered in thick brown fur, and he had delicate, pointed black hoofs instead of feet.

Astounded, Lief realized that he was looking at a being he had thought was merely a legend. The Granous had captured a Capricon.

8 - Deadly Games

The Granous pack was still shrieking and howling. Taking advantage of the noise, Lief slipped quickly through the trees, circling until he was directly behind the bound Capricon.

He took out his knife, lay down, and wriggled through the undergrowth. Soon he was pressed against the back of the tree to which the Capricon was tied.

The tree trunk was broad and hid him well, but in turn he could see nothing. The noise in the clearing was dying down. He knew he had to find out where all the Granous were before trying to cut the vines.

A straggly bush grew beside the tree. Lief eased himself to his knees. He peered cautiously around the tree, using the sparse branches of the bush as a screen.

The head Granous was squatting on the ground in front of its prisoner, arranging something in the dust.

"Very well then, creature," it cackled after a moment, shuffling back. "Are you ready for your next question?"

The Capricon moaned and struggled vainly. Lief saw that the Granous had arranged some sticks in the dust, to make a crude fish shape.

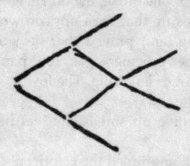

"Here is a fish from our stream," said the Granous, flexing its thin, wiry fingers. "There are precious few of them, but this is one."

The other Granous tittered.

"Now," their leader said. "This fish is swimming to the left. If it goes on doing that, it will escape our nets, and we do not want that. Do we, friends?"

"Oh, no!" chorused the other Granous, grinning hideously.

"So, creature," said the head Granous. "By moving three sticks — no more, no less — you must make our fish turn around so it is swimming to the right."

The Capricon moaned, shaking his head help-lessly.

The Granous laughed and snapped their jaws.

His mind racing, Lief eased himself back behind the tree and began sawing at the vines. They were very tough, and there were three lengths, knotted separately so that if one broke, the others would still hold.

He was sure that the Capricon would feel what he was doing, and prayed that he would make no sign. But the prisoner was too panic-stricken, it seemed, to notice anything. The low moaning did not change or falter.

"Don't give up so easily!" Lief heard the head Granous jeer.

"Please!" mumbled the Capricon. "Please . . ."

One vine was almost cut through. Leaving a few strands in place so that the bond would not fall and alert the enemy, Lief began on the next.

"You have till we count to twenty to solve the puzzle," said the Granous. "As before, if you do not solve it, the penalty is one finger. Ready? Go!"

The other Granous began to chant. "Twenty. Nineteen. Eighteen . . ."

Lief risked another glimpse around the tree.

The Capricon was gaping wildly at the diagram. Clearly he did not have the faintest idea how to solve the puzzle.

The Granous shouted and stamped. "Fourteen. Thirteen . . ."

Grinning, their leader turned and began triumphantly conducting them. Their eyes were fixed on him.

None of them are watching, Lief thought. *Now is our chance. But I will never cut these vines in time!*

He stared at the diagram, forcing himself to think.

"Ten. Nine. Eight . . ."

Then, suddenly, Lief saw the answer. Recklessly he leaned forward and whispered in the Capricon's ear. The Capricon jumped and cried out in shock.

Luckily the Granous were too busy stamping and counting to notice.

"Do as I say!" Lief whispered urgently. "Make haste!"

But the Capricon, whimpering and trembling, seemed unable to move.

"Six. Five . . ."

Abandoning all caution, Lief ducked out of cover, reached forward, and rearranged the sticks himself.

"THREE! TWO!"

Lief jerked back behind the bush with a split second to spare. The lead Granous turned around, sharp, yellow teeth grinning and snapping.

"ONE! . . . Oh!"

The pack howled in disappointment as they saw that the stick fish was now facing to the right. Shallow grooves in the dust showed where the three moved sticks had been.

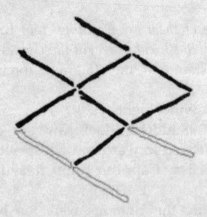

The head Granous lumbered forward. Gnawing at one of its grimy yellow nails, it stared down at the diagram. Then it looked suspiciously at the prisoner, who was cringing against the tree trunk.

"You cheated!" it accused. "The penalty for cheating is five fingers!"

"No!" the Capricon wailed, cradling his injured hand. "No, please! It wasn't my fault! It was . . ." He half-turned to look behind him.

Lief stiffened.

"Get on with the game!" shouted one of the pack.

"The game! The game!" chanted all the others.

Furiously, the head Granous kicked the sticks aside, showering the Capricon with dust.

"The next puzzle will not be so easy, creature," it

growled. Then it turned and slouched out of Lief's sight.

Lief began cutting the second vine, every now and then peeping out at the clearing.

The other Granous waited, muttering to one another in low voices. Then there was a sound from the trees at the other end of the clearing. They all swung around to look, and two went to investigate, quickly disappearing into the undergrowth.

Lief left a few strands of the second vine, to hold it in place, and began on the third. This time the Capricon felt it and whimpered.

"Be quiet!" whispered Lief, sawing desperately. "I am releasing you!"

He heard a chorus of rasping calls and again peered through the bush. The Granous had all moved to the other end of the clearing and were calling their invisible companions. When no answer came, two more lumbered into the trees.

Jasmine and Barda are doing well, Lief thought.

But there were still seven Granous in the clearing — eight, counting the leader.

Too many. Far too many to fight.

He returned to his work with new energy. When the third vine was almost cut through he moved to look through the bush once more.

The head Granous was returning with something clutched in its hand.

"I have cut the vines almost through," Lief

breathed to the Capricon. "Stay absolutely still or you will break them and alert the Granous. But when I give the signal, leap up and run!"

"I cannot run!" whimpered the prisoner. "They bit off my finger! I am in agony!"

"There will be far worse pain for you if you stay here," Lief whispered furiously. "And keep your voice down!"

The head Granous reached the tree and stood grinning at his cowering prisoner.

"One of our visitors left this trinket with us," he said with an evil grin, holding out a small wooden box, richly carved and painted in a complicated pattern of scarlet and gold. "All you have to do is open it. We humble Granous have never found the trick. But I am sure a fine, clever creature like you can do it with ease."

He leaned forward and tossed the box into the Capricon's lap.

"No!" screamed the Capricon, throwing himself violently to one side. The weakened vines snapped and fell in a tangled heap into the dust.

The Granous roared in surprise and anger. The Capricon clawed at the bush that was Lief's shelter, bending and breaking the flimsy branches.

"Save me!" he screamed. "Save me!"

Lief tried to scramble back, but the Capricon caught his cloak and held it fast, sobbing and crying.

"Enemy!" howled the Granous. It hurled itself forward, snapping and snarling.

In dismay, Lief felt wiry fingers fasten on his ankle. He was jerked backwards with such tremendous force that he could do nothing to save himself.

The next moment he was lying dazed in the clearing, with the hot, foul breath of the Granous in his face and the great weight of its body on his chest, pinning down his arms.

The rest of the pack had come running and now stood in a tight circle around their leader and his captive.

Two of them had seized the Capricon, who sagged motionless between them. His head hung down, so that Lief could see the small horns beneath his curly hair. His eyes were closed.

The head Granous bent lower, its wet, black nose snuffling in Lief's face, its tiny eyes burning with fury.

"I have seen you before," it snarled. "You are the one who calls himself king. The one who made fools of us before! Well, you will never make fools of us again, king!"

It bared its sharp, yellow teeth.

It is going to kill me here and now, Lief thought.

His numbed fingers tightened on the Belt at his waist. He focused his mind on it, and with all his strength, called on the power of the gems.

Help me!

The Granous jerked back as if it had been stung. It glared at Lief for a moment, then its eyes narrowed.

"Now I know how you escaped us the first time," it hissed. "You cheated! You are carrying powerful magic. But you will not escape again. This time you are alone, and it is twelve against one. No talisman can save you."

Only then did Lief think again of Jasmine and Barda. Were they safe? Were they even now watching from the trees, trying to think of a way to rescue him?

Stay back, he begged them silently. *There are still too many of them. I insisted on coming here. Now I must pay the penalty. But while you live there is a chance that the Belt of Deltora at least can be saved.*

The other Granous shuffled. "Four of the pack went into the trees and did not come back," one growled nervously. "If this king has enchanted them . . ."

Their leader looked up with a snarl. "His sorcery does not frighten me," it snapped. "Watch me tear out his throat!"

Then, abruptly, its eyes widened in alarm. "Beware!" it roared. "Enemies behind you!"

But already two of the shaggy beasts, the two that held the Capricon, were falling to their knees, mortally wounded.

Dark blood dripping from their weapons, Jasmine and Barda leaped back and faced the rest.

"Kill them!" roared the Granous leader.

Save them! Help me!

The Belt grew hot under Lief's hands.

There was a tearing crash in the distance, and suddenly the sky overhead was filled with birds, tens of thousands of birds. The hills echoed with their panicking cries and the sound of their frantically beating wings.

The other Granous howled and covered their faces, but their leader did not falter.

"Die, sorcerer!" it hissed. It bared its dripping teeth again, its lips drawn back so far that Lief could see its black gums.

The birds scattered. The sky darkened. There was a thundering roar. Something huge plunged downward.

The Granous leader looked up and screamed.

Lief caught a terrifying glimpse of vast golden claws, heard the beating of mighty wings.

And the Granous was plucked, shrieking, up into the sky.

9 - The Golden Eye

L ief crawled to his feet. Terrified and leaderless, the Granous pack had fled. The Capricon lay motionless in the dust. Only Barda and Jasmine remained standing in the clearing.

They staggered over to Lief, and the three clung together for a moment, deeply shaken.

"The dragon," whispered Jasmine at last. "It broke through the forest canopy, and came . . ."

"It was the Belt," Lief said. His voice sounded hollow and strange to his ears. "The Belt called to it."

As he spoke, he looked up. The topaz dragon was perched on the top of the next hill, like a bird on a tree. It was eating.

Lief shuddered.

"Do you think it will come back?" Barda muttered. "Perhaps we should — "

On the ground at their feet, the Capricon stirred and moaned. Jasmine knelt down beside him.

"We can do nothing until I have bandaged his wound," she said. "He has already lost much blood. It would be a pity if he died, since we nearly killed ourselves to save him."

Calmly she inspected the injured hand. The little finger was just a ragged stump, now once again bleeding freely. She pulled out her water flask and began to clean the wound.

Lief felt queasy, and turned away.

"He is a strange-looking being. What is he?" Jasmine asked in a low voice.

"A Capricon," said Barda. "The first I have seen with my own eyes, though I have met travelers who told of sighting small groups of them in the mountains of the east."

"Are they wanderers, then?" Jasmine asked.

Lief wondered if she was trying to keep her mind from her gruesome task with these questions.

Probably not. Jasmine was never squeamish. More likely she was trying not to think of the dragon still feasting on the next hill.

Determinedly, he turned back to face her. He, too, preferred not to think of the dragon.

"The Capricons are wanderers now," Barda said. "Those who are left. But it is said that once they lived in a rose-pink city called Capra, the most beautiful city in the east. The people of Broome claim that their city is built on Capra's ruins, but I do not know if that is true."

"I wonder why the Capricons left their home," Jasmine said as she smeared ointment on the ghastly wound and quickly began to bandage it.

"Perhaps they were driven out by servants of the Shadow Lord, as the people of the City of the Rats were," murmured Lief.

"For what purpose?" Jasmine tied the bandage firmly and sat back on her heels with a sigh.

"Who knows?" Lief said, his eyes on the dragon. "We might as well ask why the Shadow Lord wanted the City of the Rats to be abandoned. He could just as well have enslaved the people there as anywhere else."

Barda shrugged. "In any case, it is ancient history. It is said that Capra was in ruins before Adin made the Belt of Deltora, and Capricons have always held themselves apart. Little is known of them."

"Dragons," mumbled the Capricon. "Dragons took Capra from us."

His eyes fluttered open. They were a deep, violet blue, glazed with shock and confusion.

"Once the Capricons were many," he said thickly. "Once we were a great people, with a great city. But the dragons envied us. They wanted Capra for their own, because it was rich and beautiful. So they attacked again and again, killing and destroying, till at last the Capricons were driven out, and Capra was in ruins . . ."

His voice trailed off. He lifted his bandaged hand and stared at it dazedly. "I . . . I am hurt," he stammered. "How have I . . . ?"

Then his face changed as memory slowly returned. He began to tremble.

"I came from the mountains of the east, to seek help from the king," he murmured. "Help for my people . . ."

Kree landed on Jasmine's arm with a warning squawk. She looked up.

Lief glanced up, too, and his heart pounded as he saw that the dragon, its meal finished, had turned in their direction, and was spreading its wings.

"Barda," he said urgently. "You and Jasmine move into the trees. Take our friend — "

"I am Rolf," the Capricon broke in. "Rolf, eldest son of the clan Dowyn, heir to the lordship of Capra. I — "

Without ceremony, Barda hauled him up and began dragging him out of the clearing, his hoofs trailing in the dust.

Jasmine remained where she was, her eyes fixed to the sky. Filli, too, was looking up, chattering fearfully. Jasmine murmured to him, and he crept beneath her collar. But Kree stayed on her arm, still as a statue.

"Jasmine — " Lief began.

She shook her head. "I am not leaving you, Lief,"

she said. "Do not waste energy arguing with me. Be ready!"

Lief looked up again, and for a wild moment could see nothing but empty sky.

Yet the dragon was coming. He knew it. He could hear the beating of its wings. He could see the treetops thrashing and the leaves flying, as if tossed by a gale.

The clearing darkened as something blocked the sun. Lief's eyes strained as he searched for the shape he knew he must find.

Then, with a thrill of awe and terror, he saw it.

The golden dragon was hovering directly above the clearing, huge and menacing. Its whole underside was pale blue, blending perfectly with the afternoon sky, so that from below it was almost invisible.

As Lief watched, it began to sink lower, lower, its wings beating lazily, its terrible talons spread.

The Belt of Deltora seemed to throb in time to the wingbeats. Lief tore his eyes from the dragon and looked down. The topaz was gleaming like the sun.

His head was spinning. Dimly he realized that he had been holding his breath. He forced himself to breathe out, take in more air.

Dust was swirling around him. He felt Jasmine grip his arm, heard her shouting over the roaring of the wind, but he could not understand what she wanted of him.

There was a blur of black in front of him. It

was Kree screeching, wings beating on his face. And now Jasmine was in front of him, too, pushing him, screaming at him. Confused, he stumbled back, back to the edge of the clearing.

And only when he found himself pressed against the tree to which the Capricon had been bound did he realize why Jasmine had wanted him to move. Only then did he raise his head, just in time to see the vast beast land, settling onto the dust, curling its tail around its huge body, completely filling the clearing with a blinding shimmer of gold.

The dragon turned its massive head and fixed him with a golden eye. Lief felt himself captured, held. He could not look away.

"You wear the Belt of the ancients," the dragon said. "The great topaz shines for you. I feel its power flowing into me, like new blood in my veins. You are the king who was promised."

The words vibrated in Lief's ears, hollow and echoing as if rising from a deep well. He could see his own reflection in the dragon's eye, drifting there like a small, lonely creature drowning in an ancient sea.

In his mind there was no thought. Everything he had planned to say had vanished from his mind.

The dragon blinked, and the spell was broken. Suddenly freed, Lief gasped and staggered.

"I have slept long, and in my sleep I dreamed," the dragon said. "My dreams were good dreams of times as they once were, when the skies were free and the air of my domain was sweet. Now you have awoken me — to this!"

Its black, forked tongue flickered out, tasting the air. "The land is not well. I feel an evil presence, poison leaking into the earth from some dark center. Who has done this, while I slept?"

"The Enemy from the Shadowlands," Lief said huskily. "The Enemy whose creatures destroyed your race, long ago."

The flat, golden eye regarded him coldly. "My race was not destroyed," the dragon said. "Am I not here? Do you think *I* am a dream?"

Lief stared, not knowing what to say.

Thoughtfully the dragon raised a claw and picked a small piece of bone from between its sharp, white teeth.

"The topaz you wear has given me new life, but my long sleep has left my body weak," it said. "One Granous has done little to satisfy my hunger. But when I have fed well and gathered strength, I will search out this evil thing that lies in my land like a worm in a bud, and I will destroy it, if I can."

Lief's heart leaped.

"There is more than one," he said eagerly. "There are four — called the Four Sisters by the Enemy. And we already know where one of them lies. It is on the east coast, in a place called Dragon's Nest."

The dragon's eyes seemed to glaze. "The east

coast is the territory of the ruby, and not my concern," it said.

The blood rushed to Lief's face. "But surely the whole of Deltora is your concern!" he exclaimed. "As it is mine!"

The dragon's terrible jaws gaped wide. Jasmine cried out in warning and reached for her dagger. But then it became clear that the beast was only yawning.

"The territory of the ruby is not my concern," it repeated at last. "Even if I wished to enter it, I could not do so without breaking the oath I swore before I slept. And I cannot break my oath, for I swore it by my blood, and by my teeth, and by my young as yet unborn, to the man called Dragonfriend."

Hearing Lief's cry of astonishment, it seemed to smile. "Do you know of Dragonfriend?" it asked. "The one your people called the Dragonlover?"

"Of — of course!" Lief stammered. "But — "

"Seven savage enemies prowled our skies in those days," the dragon said. "Together they hunted us. They killed and killed again till at last it came to pass that I was the only one left of all my tribe. Dragonfriend came to me in my loneliness. He said that each of the other dragon tribes had suffered the same fate."

"You mean — only one dragon remained from each of the seven tribes?" Lief burst out.

The dragon moved restlessly. "So Dragonfriend

told me, and so I believed, for I had known him of old, and he had never lied to me."

The golden eye flicked in Lief's direction. Lief swallowed and nodded.

"Dragonfriend had made a plan to preserve our lives," the dragon went on. "He was wise in our ways. He knew that dragons can sleep for centuries, if they must. He said that I and the other six should hide ourselves from the Enemy and let sleep embrace us until it was safe to wake."

"But how — how would you know when it was safe?" Jasmine asked. "What was to stop you sleeping forever?"

The dragon turned its cold gaze upon her. Lief saw the flat, golden eye dwelling with interest on her flowing hair, and wished she had not spoken.

"Dragonfriend said that one day each of us would be called by the great gem of our own territory," the dragon said. "He said the call would only come when the heir of the ancient king Adin was near us, wearing the Belt of Power. For that would mean that the Shadow Lord had been defeated and his creatures banished from our skies."

"So the seven of you slept," Lief breathed. "And — you each swore not to take advantage of another's sleep to invade its land."

"That is so," said the dragon. "And I will not break my oath. If you wish to seek the evil at Dragon's

Nest, you must rouse the dragon of the ruby to help you."

"But what if the ruby dragon cannot be found?" Lief asked desperately. "What if it is unwilling? Or dead? Will you come to me then?"

The dragon closed its eyes. After a long moment it opened them again. "If it cannot be found, or if it is unwilling, the oath to Dragonfriend must stand. If it is dead . . . then we shall see."

10 – A Change of Plans

Night was falling by the time Lief, Jasmine, and Barda half-carried Rolf the Capricon out of the Os-Mine foothills and back to their camp. Even on the plain, the howls of Granous being hunted by the ravenous dragon drifted on the air. The companions were not surprised to find the horses snorting and restless and the guards huddled together over a huge fire, weapons and torches at the ready.

From the shelter of the trees around the clearing, Rolf had caught a glimpse of the dragon. From that moment he had retreated into shocked silence. The pain from his wounded hand and the ghastly cries that had rung in their ears on their downward trek had made matters worse.

Now his eyes were glassy, he trembled continually, and his legs seemed to have lost the power to support him. He paid no attention at all to the curious stares of the guards as he was helped into the camp.

"Put him by the fire," Jasmine said in a low voice. "I will make a brew to ease his pain."

"If it will make him sleep, too, all the better," Barda muttered. "I do not want him babbling of dragons to the men. They are nervous enough as it is."

The guards, mightily relieved to have their chief and their king back safely, and satisfied with Barda's mutterings of noisy wolves in the Hills, settled to preparing their meal.

The Capricon drank half a cup of the herbal tea Jasmine held to his lips, and fell into an exhausted sleep. At last, the sounds from the Hills died away.

"Our scaly friend seems to have decided it has eaten enough for one day," Barda said, slumping down in front of the fire with his companions.

"It is just too dark for it to see its prey," Jasmine said. "That beast did not look to me as if it would ever have enough of feasting."

"What will happen, then, when it has eaten all the Granous in the Hills?" growled Barda.

Lief felt a chill, but shook his head determinedly. "There are many Granous," he said. "They bred to plague proportions while the dragon slept."

"Perhaps. But who is to say it does not like to vary its diet sometimes?" said Jasmine. "Remember the story of Capra. And I did not like the way it looked at me in the clearing. If you had not been present with the Belt, I am sure it would have made short work of me."

"I think it only wanted your hair to line its nest," Lief murmured. "What a strange story it told. I can still hardly believe it."

"I would be pleased at least to have the chance to try," Barda said drily. "I was in the trees minding a trembling Capricon while you spoke to the beast, and I heard nothing. But as we are here, and it is still up there, I gather it has refused to help us."

"It is more complicated than that," Lief said.

He told the dragon's story, and Barda listened carefully, all the while playing with the little locked box he had picked up before leaving the clearing.

"So Doran persuaded the last dragons to sleep," he said when Lief had finished. "Then, traveling back to Del, perhaps, he began hearing whispers of the Four Sisters. But by then it was too late. The dragons would not wake, even for him."

He sighed, turning the carved box over in his hands, pressing it here and there, trying to find the hidden lock that would open it.

"No wonder Doran's last note in the *Annals* was so desperate," he said. "He must have felt that he actually helped the Enemy by removing the last barriers to his plan."

Jasmine shrugged. "If he thought that, he was wrong. There was only one dragon left in each territory. They would have been killed by the Ak-Baba, one by one, if they had tried to interfere."

"Unless the Belt was with them," Lief said slowly.

He was remembering words he had seen in the *Deltora Annals* — words scrawled in desperation, long ago, by Doran's hand:

> Whoever reads my words, show them to the King if you can. The King, wearing the Belt of Deltora, is Deltora's only salvation now.

Lief looked down at the Belt — at the great topaz gleaming with strange new depth and life. The golden dragon had added to its power. And the topaz had added to the dragon's power. He was certain that it would be the same with the ruby — if they could find the ruby dragon.

If...

He felt inside his jacket for the Dragon Territories map Josef had given him. Carefully he unfolded it and spread it out so his friends could see it.

"We had planned to move back south after this, then travel east to Dragon's Nest by the coast road," he said, rapidly tracing the path with his finger. "But if we take that way we will not cross into the territory of the ruby until we have almost reached our goal."

"Does that matter?" asked Jasmine.

"I think so," Lief said. "We do not know where

the ruby dragon sleeps, but surely the less of its land we cover, the less are our chances of finding it."

Barda nodded slowly. "You think, then, that we should move northeast," he said. "That will take us into ruby territory almost at once. But it is a longer way. Unless you plan to lead this parade of ours through the Forests of Silence — which would surely be madness!"

"The Forests are not so bad, if you keep to the trees and stay alert," Jasmine said stoutly.

"With you as our guide, Jasmine, the three of us alone could try it," Lief agreed. "But Barda is right. Our present party is far too large to risk such a dangerous shortcut."

He put the map away and stretched, suddenly aware of how weary he was. "We had better eat now, and get some sleep," he said. "Barda, will you tell Brid we leave at dawn?"

"A little before dawn, I think," said Barda, giving up on the locked box and thrusting it into his pocket in annoyance. "Whatever you say, Lief, I want to be well away from here by the time that dragon begins hunting again."

＊

The next two days were long and filled with frustration. The weakness of Rolf the Capricon, who was mounted unsteadily on a spare horse led by Barda, slowed their pace to a walk. Also, once the Os-Mine

Hills were behind them, the travelers began to encounter farms and villages.

Seeing the string of riders approaching, people ran out to greet them, overjoyed at this unexpected visit from their king, thrilled to see the heroes Jasmine and Barda, impressed by the guards, and fascinated by the Capricon.

The people were tired and worn, exhausted by the effort of toiling in barren fields while at the same time trying to rebuild houses destroyed in the time of the Shadow Lord. Many had been prisoners in the Shadowlands, and had only recently been restored to their homes.

It was impossible to disappoint them. Impossible to refuse their pleas to stay a while, to share what food and drink they could provide, in the way of the country.

But even as his heart bled for them, Lief fretted over the hours that slipped by as he inspected the work they had managed to complete, and sympathized over failed crops and scrawny herds.

What was worse, as he and his party ate the stringy chicken, wizened apples, and hard bread put before them, he was uneasily aware that the food could not really be spared.

The travelers always left a parting gift of food from their own supplies when at last they were allowed to leave, but Lief knew it could not make up for the feast they had been served. He knew that the villagers would be even hungrier as a result of the royal visit.

"If only we did not have the guards with us," he murmured as they rode away from yet another cheering crowd on the third day. "They make our group so large that we cannot go anywhere unnoticed."

"They are our official escort," said Barda, turning in his saddle to wave at a pair of skinny, redheaded children who were running after them, trying to keep up with the horses. "We cannot send them home without raising suspicion in Del that our reason for this journey is not what we claimed. Rumors will start. People will panic. And that is exactly what we do not want."

He glanced at Lief's dismal face. "Do not despair," he said. "By my calculation we are about to enter the territory of the ruby. Keep your eyes on the Belt. We must not risk passing the ruby dragon by."

Lief nodded and straightened his back, ashamed of his gray mood. He glanced down at the Belt. The topaz still glowed, but the ruby was dull pink instead of the shining red it should be.

Danger. Danger here or approaching.

He looked warily from side to side, and then behind him, but could see nothing. The road was deserted. Even the red-haired twins had disappeared. He guessed they had grown tired of the chase, and had run back to the village.

"Another road crosses this one not far ahead," exclaimed Jasmine, standing up on her stirrups and shading her eyes. "But there is a signpost."

They reached the signpost not long afterwards. It was battered and faded, and bent forward a little as though exhausted by its long years of service.

"Ah, good, Ringle!" Barda said with satisfaction. "It is on our way. I thought it would be marked. It is quite a large town, or used to be."

"Another town! At this rate, we will never reach Dragon's Nest," Jasmine muttered as they turned their horses' heads to the right and plodded on. "Of course, all these stops would not matter so much if only we could move faster when we were actually on the road."

Lief glanced back at Rolf, who was already slumped forward. "Rolf slows us sadly, I know, but we cannot leave him to be cared for by the farmers here," he said in a low voice. "They do not have enough to feed themselves! And he is still far too weak to be left alone."

"He could be strong if he wished!" snapped Jasmine, taking no trouble to keep her voice down. "He eats and sleeps well enough, and his wound is healing. He puts all his energy into pitying himself."

"He has lost his nerve," Barda said. "I have seen it happen to soldiers who have suffered sorely in battle. The sight of the dragon was too much for him."

"*Everything* is too much for him!" Jasmine retorted. "I doubt he had any nerve to lose."

"Do not argue," Lief begged, feeling that his own nerves could take no more. "At present we have no choice but to go on as we are. We may as well make the best of it, and hope that something happens to change things soon."

Not long after that something *did* happen. But not at all the sort of thing he expected.

11 - Signs of Trouble

The road quickly narrowed to a rough, winding path. After more than an hour there was still no sign of Ringle or its outlying farms.

The ground on the left of the path began to fall away steeply. At last, the travelers found themselves being forced to ride in single file, with a steep, rocky hill on one side and a jagged chasm on the other.

Lief reined in Honey and called a halt. "I think someone must have tampered with that signpost at the crossroads," he called, looking down at the fearsome drop on his left. "This is surely not the way to Ringle."

"I agree," Barda rumbled from behind him. "I fear we have been led to End Wood Gap. The post was leaning badly. No doubt it was loosened when it was turned around."

"But who would do such a thing?" exclaimed Jasmine in irritation.

Barda shrugged. "Some lout with a tiny brain, who thought it amusing to mislead travelers."

But Lief was not sure it was as simple as that. The ruby and the emerald in the Belt of Deltora were still as dull as river stones. His skin prickled with the awareness of danger, with the feeling that someone or something was wishing him ill.

On an impulse, he lowered his hand and pressed his fingers against the ruby. He shut his eyes and with all his strength thought of the ruby dragon.

"Wherever you are sleeping, dragon, awake!" he whispered. "I summon you! The Belt of Deltora summons you!"

He opened his eyes. Nothing had changed. Nothing moved on the rocky hill, or in the chasm. The sky was blank and empty.

"We will go back," he muttered. Impatiently he tried to turn Honey around, but the horse reared and snorted in terror as the earth at the edge of the narrow path crumbled under her hoofs.

Jasmine, Barda, Rolf, and the guards shouted with one voice. Dirt and stones showered to the depths below.

Lief held on grimly, turning Honey's head to face the front once more, urging her on till she found sure footing and at last stood trembling but safe on firm ground.

Sick with relief he patted her, speaking to her softly, cursing his own foolishness.

"It is not safe to turn the horses here," said Barda unnecessarily. Lief turned in the saddle to glance at him. The big man's face was beaded with sweat.

At a word from Jasmine, Kree took flight. He soared upward, made a great circle above their heads, and moments later was back, squawking harshly.

"Kree says that ahead there is a bridge over the Gap," Jasmine said, ignoring the fascinated stares of the guards.

The straggling group moved on again. Sure enough, just around the next bend, where the gap narrowed a little, a rickety wooden bridge straddled the sickening drop. A roughly painted sign stood beside it.

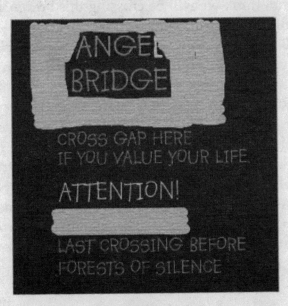

ANGEL BRIDGE

CROSS GAP HERE
IF YOU VALUE YOUR LIFE.

ATTENTION!

LAST CROSSING BEFORE
FORESTS OF SILENCE

The companions looked at the sign in silence, then glanced at one another. Barda raised his eyebrows. Lief and Jasmine nodded.

"So that is how it is," said Barda grimly.

Lief bit his lip. "Yes," he said. "I have feared it for some time. This is the proof."

By now the guards at the head of the troop had seen the sign, and the dreaded words "Forests of Silence" were passing in whispers down the line. Rolf had shrunk down in his saddle, his eyes wide and fearful.

"We will have to lead the horses across, sir," Brid called to Barda. "They will need coaxing. Will I tell the men to dismount?"

"No," Barda growled, without turning around. "I do not think we will be crossing this bridge. I think we will be going on."

Brid sat rigidly, eyes straight ahead. He was plainly dismayed, but was too well trained to complain about his chief's order.

Rolf, however, gave a high, strangled cry. "We *cannot* go on!" he squealed. "You cannot lead us into the Forests of Silence to die!"

Barda swung down from his horse. He strode to the sign and ran his fingers over it thoughtfully.

As his men watched intently he pulled his large hunting knife from his belt. Then, gently but firmly, he began to scrape the face of the sign.

Curls of gleaming white paint fell to the ground

as he worked. And when he stood aside, the guards gasped.

"So," Barda said, rubbing his knife on his leggings to remove the shreds of paint still clinging to the blade. "It is as we thought. Not content with leading us astray, someone painted over the bridge sign to try to put an end to us. It is fortunate that this was done so recently, and so clumsily, that we saw through the trick at once. Otherwise . . ."

Frowning, he sheathed his knife and picked up a large rock. He threw the rock onto the first few planks of the bridge. The bridge groaned, but held firm.

Barda lifted another rock. This time he threw it further, so that it landed towards the bridge's center.

At once, several rotten timbers gave way, the bridge jolted and sagged, and the rock plummeted down, smashing into pieces on the ground far below.

There were muffled groans as everyone present imagined what would have happened if Lief, Barda, and Jasmine had led the way across the bridge. Nothing was said as Barda remounted his horse.

The party plodded on, this time with the companions in the lead. Rolf and the guards turned often, looking back at the ruined bridge until it was out of sight. But Lief, Barda, and Jasmine did not look back at all. They were talking together in low voices.

If any were curious about their conversation, that curiosity remained unsatisfied. Barda had let the lead rein on Rolf's horse out as far as it would go, creating a gap between the three and all their followers, so no one could hear what they said.

✳

Gradually the Gap became narrower, and in time, as the sign had promised, the travelers reached another bridge.

Here the path ended, and not far ahead the Gap was swallowed up by a forbidding mass of trees. All guessed that this was End Wood, the last of the three Forests of Silence.

On the other side of the bridge a narrow road wound away into the distance. The bridge itself looked sturdy and almost new. A carved stone stood proudly beside it.

"Now listen carefully," said Barda, raising his voice so everyone could hear. "Twice, signs on our path have been altered. We believe these were deliberate attempts to injure us. We have decided, therefore, that our party should separate, for the safety of all."

Rolf made a small sound of protest, then clapped his hand over his mouth. The guards stared.

"Under Brid's command, you are to go to the outskirts of Ringle," Barda went on. "There, without troubling the citizens, you will make camp for the night. Then you will move on to Broome. Is that understood?"

Brid cleared his throat. "What of you, sir?" he

asked. "You, and the lady Jasmine, and the king?"

"We will also go to Broome," Barda said evenly. "But we will go on foot, and by another way."

Every man's eyes turned to the forest ahead. Every face filled with dread. Rolf clutched his heart and began to wail.

"But what of me?" he howled. "What of me?"

"You will go with the guards," said Lief quickly, hearing Jasmine draw breath for a sharp retort. "You will be perfectly safe, Rolf, I promise. Is that not so, Brid?"

Brid nodded, his scarred face wooden.

"Then let us waste no more time." Barda clapped Brid on the shoulder. "Keep safe," he said.

"And you, sir," muttered Brid. A nerve high on his cheek twitched, but he pressed his lips together and said no more. He turned to his men and began to give orders.

In moments, the guards were moving across the bridge. Brid, leading Rolf's horse, was at their head. Honey, Bella, and Swift, on lead ropes, trailed at the rear.

Lief sighed with relief as the whole party reached the other side in safety. He saw the men turn and wave in farewell, and raised his own arm in response.

"I hope we are doing the right thing," Barda muttered. "Brid clearly thinks we are mad."

Jasmine snorted. "Brid thinks anything out of the ordinary is mad," she said. "He is so dull!"

"Brid survived ten years as a slave in the Shadowlands," Barda said quietly. "No doubt this made him thoughtful."

Jasmine bit her lip. "I did not mean to insult him," she said. "But you should not let his disapproval shake you, Barda. This is our best chance of losing our enemy and reaching Broome without endless delays."

She sighed. "It is a pity we had to let the horses go, but we had no choice. Horses cannot sleep in trees as we can."

Filli chattered agreement, delighted to be rid of the large creatures that had jolted him about so painfully.

Barda groaned. The idea of sleeping in the fork of a tree did not appeal to him at all.

Lief said nothing. He was startled to find that, despite everything, he was feeling extremely happy.

Am I as mad as Brid thinks? he wondered. *There is nothing to be happy about!*

But he *was* happy. Yes, he was worried by what had passed. Yes, he knew that danger lay ahead. But as for the present — why, he felt like singing as he stood with Jasmine and Barda, watching the guards move away.

Watching the guards move away . . .

And that, he thought suddenly, *must be the answer*.

The guards were always very respectful to him. They regarded him with awe. But this did not please him. Instead, it made him feel like a fraud. It made him terribly aware of just how young he was, in comparison to them. And it made him feel that he had to act like a king at all times, so he wouldn't shock or disappoint them.

Now, however, with only Jasmine and Barda for company, he could be himself. He was free.

He felt as if his blood was fizzing in his veins. As if the air was sweeter and the colors in the world brighter than they had been before.

"Come on!" he shouted. And began running towards the Forest.

12 ~ End Wood

After several hours of walking, Lief's bubbling happiness had settled to a feeling of quiet contentment. The twisted, weed-choked trees of the Forest fringe had been left behind. End Wood was now a beautiful place, filled with birdsong. Golden pools of sunlight dappled the soft earth, and ferns clustered at the roots of the mighty trees.

All the companions knew, however, that the evil reputation of the Forests of Silence was well deserved. They knew, too, that within the greatest beauty terror could be lying in wait. So they walked in silence, one behind the other, alert for signs of danger.

Just before sunset, Jasmine chose a tree for them, and they climbed up to high branches where they could eat and sleep in some safety.

It was not a restful night. They dozed fitfully in turns as unseen creatures slid and prowled below them. In the darkest hours, when the moon had set, a faint, chilling chorus of howls and screams began. It lasted only a few minutes, but after it had died away, the companions slept no more.

They welcomed the dawn gratefully, but forced themselves to wait until sunlight fell on the forest floor before venturing down from their hiding place and moving on.

As before, Jasmine led them, threading her way almost silently through the trees, brushing the smooth bark of each one lightly with the tips of her fingers as she passed. Kree fluttered ahead of her, a black shadow against a background of green and gold.

After a time, Jasmine began to move faster. Lief and Barda, their muscles stiff and aching after their night in the tree, found themselves struggling to keep her in view.

"Jasmine, slow down!" Lief called in a low voice. But Jasmine only turned with a frown, her finger to her lips, beckoned impatiently, and set off again, even faster than before.

At last Lief became aware that a new sound had begun to mingle with the birdsong. It was the sound of trickling water — a stream, somewhere near.

It made him realize how thirsty he was, but he did not dare to stop and drink from his water flask. Jasmine was almost running now, and all he could do was follow.

The gurgling, rippling sound grew louder, and at last Jasmine stopped.

Lief saw that she had reached the stream he had been listening to for so long. Broad and shallow, the stream ran directly across their path, sunbeams dancing on the clear water that gurgled over its pebbled bed.

On the other side of the stream there were no trees, only a mass of giant ferns, rising like a feathery barrier that completely hid whatever was beyond.

Kree fluttered down to the water's edge. Jasmine waited while he drank. Only when he had finished, and had flown up to perch on a branch high above her head, did she kneel to drink herself.

Filli scuttled down from her shoulder and began to drink also. His tiny pink tongue lapped busily, but all the time his dark eyes darted from side to side, so he could not be taken by surprise.

"Did you have to go so fast?" Barda muttered as he and Lief at last reached the stream and crouched beside Jasmine to quench their raging thirsts.

"The trees say we are being followed," Jasmine said shortly. "Someone has been tracking us since dawn, from the direction of End Wood Gap."

As she spoke she glanced up to where Kree kept watch. He was so still that he looked part of the tree itself. Only his yellow eye was moving, fierce and bright.

Lief had lifted a handful of water to his lips. Now he felt as if the icy liquid was trickling down his spine.

He glanced down at the Belt. The topaz still gleamed brightly, but the ruby had paled once more.

"Who?" he murmured.

Jasmine lifted Filli to her shoulder, wiped her mouth with the back of her hand, and stood up.

"The same enemy, I imagine, who tried to make us fall to our deaths at End Wood Gap," she said. "All the trees can tell me is that he is tall and fierce, and moving much faster than we are. Where we have traveled above ground, he does also, swinging from tree to tree. Where we have gone on foot, he runs bent double, sniffing the ground like a beast."

The words painted a disturbing picture. Lief's scalp crawled.

"How close is he now?" Barda asked. Once, the big man had scoffed at the idea that Jasmine could understand the language of trees, but those days were long past.

"Already he has almost reached the place where we spent the night," Jasmine said. "We must throw him off the scent. That is why I made haste to reach the stream. If we wade through the water he will not be able to smell our tracks. He will not know if we have gone left or right, and so we may escape him."

"Why should we try to escape?" Barda growled. "Why not stand and face him? I would like to give him proper thanks for all he has done for us." Scowling, he touched his sword.

"We took this way to save time, Barda," Jasmine pointed out coldly. "The forest edge cannot be far away now. Do we want to waste energy fighting a beast-man who has a grudge against us? Or do we want to reach Dragon's Nest with all speed?"

"We want to reach Dragon's Nest," Lief said reluctantly. "Let us use the stream, as Jasmine says."

He felt as Barda did, but he knew that Jasmine's plan was more practical. To Jasmine, all that mattered was the task at hand. Pride, revenge, curiosity . . . to her, such things were not important, and could wait.

And they can *wait — of course they can*, Lief told himself. But secretly he sympathized as Barda grumbled in annoyance.

Jasmine stepped into the stream and waded a little way along it to the right. She touched the violets often with her hands and let her hair tangle with the ferns that overhung the water's edge. Then she turned, tucked her hair beneath her collar, flattened herself in the water, and crawled back, being careful to touch nothing.

"That should lead him astray very well," she grinned. "Now follow me. Keep in the center of the stream and very low, so that the ferns do not brush your backs."

She set off towards the left, following her own advice. Lief and Barda crawled after her.

They moved through the cold water for what seemed like a very long time. Lief's hands were numb and his teeth were chattering when Jasmine at last called a halt.

"I think we have gone far enough now," she whispered, getting to her feet. "And see here!"

She pointed at the bank beside her. There, to his amazement, Lief saw a pathway of large, rounded stones winding away through the ferns.

"It must be the bed of another stream that once joined this one," Jasmine said. "If our luck holds, it will at least lead us through the ferns — and perhaps all the way to the forest edge."

"Anything to get off our knees and out of this cursed water!" muttered Barda, crawling to his feet.

Shivering, the companions waded out of the stream and began following the mossy path.

Soon it was as if they were moving through a soft green tunnel. Great, arching fronds met over their heads so they could not see the sky.

The air was thick with the smell of damp earth and rotting leaves. There was not a breath of wind, and no birds sang. They walked with their hands on the hilts of their weapons, not speaking, barely breathing.

Lief glanced down. He could not rid himself of the idea that there was something very odd about the path.

He tried to convince himself that Jasmine was right, and it was an old stream bed. Yet the stones were so large and so evenly placed — almost as if someone had gathered them and put them on the path, one by one.

But who would have done such a thing? And for what purpose, in this wilderness?

"Oh!"

Lief's head jerked up as Jasmine gasped, and his sword was in his hand before he realized that she was not in danger.

She was standing stock-still, holding a feathery veil of ferns apart, staring at something ahead.

"Look!" she breathed.

Lief and Barda crowded in behind her and peered over her shoulder . . . at something that was like a picture in a book of fairy tales.

Beyond the ferns, countless small trees loaded with golden fruits grew in a broad pool of still, shallow water. They were perfectly reflected in the water's mirror-like surface, their graceful trunks rising, their broad green leaves spreading, their fruits glowing like tiny, floating suns.

Jasmine moved forward.

"Wait, Jasmine!" Barda called urgently. "Wait! We do not know . . ."

But Jasmine had already stepped into the water. It barely reached her ankles. She turned her head, smiling.

"It is warm," she said. "Oh, and see the fruit! Can you smell it?"

Lief could indeed smell the fruit. It was a glorious, rich, sweet scent. His mouth began to water.

Kree flew from Jasmine's shoulder and perched on a bough of the nearest tree. Greedily he dug his beak into one of the golden fruits.

Juice dripped into the water, making circles of ripples where it fell. The delicious fragrance grew stronger.

Filli began to whimper and chatter. Jasmine splashed to the tree and let the little creature leap up beside Kree.

The golden fruits were as big as Filli himself, but that did not dismay him. He clutched one with his paws and began nibbling it eagerly.

This was too much for Lief. He stepped into the water and moved to Jasmine's side.

"Do the trees say the fruit is safe to eat?" he murmured.

Jasmine shrugged. "These trees speak only to one another, and keep their secrets," she said. "But Filli and Kree seem sure that all is well."

Lief stretched out his hand and picked one of the fruits. It was shaped a little like a pear, but much larger and heavier. In places its smooth golden skin was slightly flushed with pink.

He lifted it to his nose and breathed in the delicious fragrance.

Then, almost without intending to do it, he took a bite.

112

13 - Sweet and Sour

A glorious taste filled Lief's mouth. Sweet, golden juice ran down his chin. Then suddenly he realized that something very bitter was mingling with the sweetness.

Quickly he spat what remained of the chewed skin into his hand, grimacing.

"The skin is bitter," he said, wrinkling his nose. "Oh! It is disgusting! How can Filli and Kree bear it?"

Jasmine grinned and pulled out her knife. "They are not as fussy about food as we are," she said. "I am glad you made the experiment before me."

She took a fruit from the tree and began to peel it. In moments she was sinking her teeth into sweet, gleaming golden flesh, murmuring with pleasure.

Lief followed her example. And after a few moments of watching suspiciously, Barda did the same.

Soon each one of them was silently absorbed in

the blissful enjoyment of a rare feast. The water around their feet was littered with fruit skins and the long, flat seeds they found in the fruits' centers.

Time passed. The sun was high in the sky. Lief, warm and full, crouched to rest his pleasantly aching legs.

He closed his eyes and began daydreaming of telling the hungry people in the villages about this rich supply of food growing at their very doorstep.

Once they know about it, they can come and gather the fruit each year, he thought lazily. *Perhaps they can even flood a field or two, and grow their own trees from the seed. How wonderful that would be! How wonderful . . .*

He became aware that Kree had begun squawking, and Filli was chattering shrilly. His brow creased in annoyance. Why were they disturbing him with their noise?

He opened his eyes, and it was then that he realized, with mild surprise, that he was not crouching any longer, but lying on his back in the water.

How strange, he thought. But he smiled, and did not try to move. The water was warm. There were a few large stones buried in the soft mud on which he lay, but they were pleasantly round and smooth.

Like the ones on the path, he thought dreamily, pushing his hand through the mud to touch a stone with his fingers.

As he stroked its warm smoothness, it came into his mind that the stones on the path could have been taken from beneath this soft, warm water. They could have been taken and used by someone who wanted to mark a trail to this place, so that creatures great and small would come here, see the beauty, taste the fruit.

Someone. Or something . . .

The thought drifted into the golden haze of Lief's mind like a small dark cloud.

He wanted to brush it away. He was so sleepy, so very comfortable . . .

But Filli was shrieking now. And he could hear Kree's cries, and the beating of his wings.

Making an enormous effort to rouse himself, Lief turned his head towards the sound. He saw Jasmine and Barda lying motionless not far away. Their hair floated like weed in the water. Their eyes were closed, their faces peaceful. Their chests were gently rising and falling.

They were deeply asleep. But how was that possible? For Kree was flapping wildly around Jasmine's head, screeching, his wing tips brushing her face.

He is trying to wake her, Lief thought dreamily. *Poor Kree.*

Then he lifted his eyes and saw something moving through the trees towards them.

It was a giant bird, as tall as the trees, with a snowy white chest, neck, and head, and black wings.

Silently, unhurriedly, the bird stalked through

the water on long orange legs, delicately lifting one foot then the other, barely stirring the mirror-like surface.

Its fixed, glassy eyes looked as if they had been painted on to its head. Its neck was like a smooth, white snake. Its orange beak was like a sword.

Lief tried to shout. But his tongue was thick and heavy, and his throat seemed swollen. The only sound he could make was a rasping groan.

And he could not move. His limbs felt as if they were fixed in the mud of the lake bed.

The Belt. The diamond . . . for strength.

Sweat broke out on his brow as he forced his left hand up to his waist. His fingers moved with agonizing slowness to the diamond beside the clasp as his terrified eyes watched the bird reach Jasmine's side.

Kree flew at the giant, screeching and pecking, but it took no more notice of him than Kree would have taken of a sparrow.

It put its head on one side and regarded the helpless girl with cold interest. Then, without haste, it dipped its sword-like beak into the water and began sharpening it on a stone.

Lief felt a thrill of fear. His fingertips touched the diamond. A tingling rose up his arm, spread through his body. It was as if strength was battling weakness in his veins.

A stone. Throw a stone.

Lief forced his sluggish fingers to curl around the stone they had been caressing. He pulled, and the stone eased out of the mud with a wet, sucking sound.

It came to the surface, mud-streaked and streaming with water. And then he saw what it was.

It was a human skull. Mud clogged its grinning jaws. Long, thin worms dangled from its eye sockets and fell squirming back into the water.

Instinctively Lief recoiled, dropping the hideous thing with a splash.

The next instant, his mind was flooded with terrified understanding.

They had been lured to a killing ground. Like so many before them they had eaten the glorious fruit that made them sleep.

So that at its leisure the giant bird which lived among the trees could come, with its stealthy tread, its snaking neck.

So that the bird could kill and feed, the bones of its prey sinking at last into the soft, warm mud of its domain.

Later, much later, picked clean by worms, polished by the muddy water, the skulls could be used to decorate the path. To make it even wider and more inviting.

The bird lifted its beak from the water and raised

it over Jasmine's body. One downward jerk of its head, and the dripping, razor-sharp point would plunge deep into Jasmine's heart.

With a strangled cry Lief heaved himself onto his side, picked up the skull again, and threw it wildly.

The skull bounced harmlessly against the giant bird's snowy breast and splashed into the water. The bird paused and tilted its head. Its unblinking eye stared at Lief without expression.

Perhaps it was wondering why this prey was moving. Or perhaps there was no thought in its mind at all.

As Lief scrabbled clumsily for another weapon, as Kree swooped and screeched around its head, it turned back to Jasmine and raised its beak again.

A blur of gray streaked from a branch beside it, and suddenly something was clinging to its long, white neck.

It was Filli — Filli as Lief had never seen him, fur standing up in spikes, tiny white teeth bared. The next instant, Filli had attacked, biting deeply. A bright spot of blood appeared on the white feathers.

Instantly the neck writhed, the head turned, and the long, sharp beak stabbed viciously.

Soundlessly Filli fell. He splashed into the water and struggled there, a small, feebly moving bundle of draggled gray fur.

The giant bird looked down at him, then lifted a huge, clawed foot to stamp him into the mud.

Lief's fingers closed around a long bone. He tore it from its soggy bed and threw it. The bone spun through the air and hit the raised foot.

This time the bird felt pain. It made a deep, rattling sound and its foot clenched. Again it turned its head, and again it fixed Lief with its cold gaze.

The feathers on the back of its neck rose in sharp quills. It lowered its bruised foot and began stalking towards him. Plainly it had decided that Lief had become a nuisance.

Lief struggled to rise, struggled to cry out, but his body was still heavy, so heavy, and still he could make no sound but harsh, gasping groans. He had another bone in his hand, but it was small and useless. His sword was pinned beneath him. Even with the help of the diamond, he could not find the strength to pull it free.

The bird looked down at him with blank eyes. It raised its beak to strike.

Then suddenly there was a roar from the bank of the lake and a spear flew over Lief's body, grazing the bird's black wing before plunging into the water behind it.

The bird faltered, took a step back. The quills on its neck rose further. Its beak opened.

The roar came again, and then there was the

sound of splashing as someone ran through the water towards them.

"On your way, Orchard Keeper!" boomed a voice. "These people are mine!"

Another spear hurtled through the air, this time scratching the bird's neck.

The bird decided it had had enough. It turned and began stalking rapidly away. In moments it had disappeared among the trees.

There was a peal of mocking laughter. A shadow fell across Lief's face. He looked up, dazed and squinting.

An enormous figure in a cap of fur towered over him, blocking the sun. An arm stretched out to pluck the spears from the mud.

"That was a near thing," boomed the voice. "One moment more and you would have been dead meat. I have been tracking you since first light — but what a dance you led me with that trick in the stream! If the black bird had not screeched fit to crack the heavens I would never have found you."

Lief struggled, and tried vainly to speak.

Again the booming laugh rang out. The shadow moved. Long legs bound with strips of leather stepped over Lief.

Lief watched in confusion as the giant stranger lifted Filli from the water, inspected him, sniffed his wet fur, then nodded and placed him gently on Jasmine's chest.

"Who . . . are . . . you?" Lief rasped.

"Why, has your sight grown as feeble as your voice, Lief of Del? Do you not know me?" roared the stranger, tearing off the fur cap.

Relief and amazement swept over Lief as he focused on the long, narrow black eyes, the straight black brows, and, most unmistakable of all, the shaved head painted with swirling red designs.

"Lindal!" he rasped. "Lindal of Broome! But how . . . ? Why . . . ? . . . Oh, it is so good to see you!"

"You will not think so when you hear the news I bring," Lindal said grimly. "But that will have to wait. First I must get you and your foolish friends on your feet. We must leave here, and I cannot carry you all."

She splashed to the nearest tree and picked a golden fruit. Then she returned to Lief and squatted beside him.

"Eat this!" she ordered, tearing off some of the fruit's skin and pressing it into Lief's mouth.

He choked and tried to spit the bitter stuff out.

"No!" Lindal shouted, pressing her hand to his lips. "Chew and swallow! Do you want to lie in this boneyard croaking like a frog forever? The skin is the antidote to Sleeper Fruit flesh. You must have eaten some before, or you would be as helpless as your friends."

When she saw that Lief had understood, she removed her hand and stood up.

"Now for the others," she said, grinning at the faces he made as he chewed the vile-tasting peel. "I will have to feed them the antidote little by little — at least until they begin to stir. When you can stand, come and help me. The bird may return in a dangerous mood, and I do not want to have to fight it to the death. It is bad luck, they say, to kill an Orchard Keeper."

14 - A Message in Blood

By the time Jasmine and Barda had been revived, the sun was low in the sky. All three of the companions were weak, and Filli was dazed and helpless, but Lindal insisted they move on.

"It is not far to the forest edge from here," she said. "When we are in the open, you can rest in safety."

Refusing to say another word, she set off at a brisk pace.

Lief, Barda, and Jasmine had no choice but to follow her. With Kree flying ahead and Filli lying limp beneath Jasmine's shirt, they beat their way through a tangle of ferns, then through thickets of brush and brambles, their legs trembling, their heads spinning.

At last, at sunset, they burst into open ground. Ahead was a vast plain. The sky was streaked red and orange. A fresh breeze cooled their faces.

They stood, exhausted and staring.

"This is my country," Lindal said with satisfaction. "Sit! Rest! I will build a fire and hunt for some food."

And so tired were Lief, Barda, and Jasmine that they crumpled to the ground where they stood.

When they woke, the sky above them was like black velvet sprinkled with diamonds. The fire had died down to a mass of glowing coals, and the air was filled with the smell of cooking.

Lindal was already eating, sitting cross-legged and chewing on a bone with relish.

When she saw that her companions had awoken, she tossed the bone aside. She licked her fingers, then seized a wicked-looking knife and began sawing at the joint of meat still sizzling on the coals.

"Here," she said, passing hot, dripping chunks to each of them. "Pig rat — a fine, plump one, too, for once."

Even Jasmine, who rarely ate meat, fell upon the food, which was rich and savory, despite its doubtful name. There was warm, flat bread, too, baked in the ashes of the fire, and some fresh, curly green leaves Lief had never seen before. They tasted slightly peppery, but were crisp and strangely refreshing.

"Traveler's Weed. Good for the belly!" said Lindal, cramming a handful of leaves into her mouth with one hand and slapping her flat stomach with the other. "I was lucky to find it. There is little around these days, though once, the old folk say, it grew in every ditch."

Her heartiness sounded a little forced, and Lief suddenly remembered what she had said about having bad news. He realized she was delaying the moment when she would have to tell it.

He leaned forward, but before he could say anything, Barda spoke.

"What a meal, Lindal!" the big man said. "How our guards would envy us! No doubt they are making a miserable dinner of traveler's biscuit and dried fish tonight."

Lindal looked stricken.

Here it comes, Lief thought, with sudden dread. *It is something about the guards.*

The smile faded from Barda's face. "What is it?" he demanded. "Why do you look like that?"

"There is something I must tell you," Lindal muttered. "Something bad. Your men . . ."

She bent her head and rubbed her hand over her painted skull. Then she looked up and met Barda's eyes.

"Your men are all dead," she said.

Jasmine gasped with shock. Barda's face looked as if it had been turned to stone.

"How?" Lief heard himself asking, and wondered how his voice could sound so calm when his mind was roaring with grief and horror.

"Their camp on the outskirts of Ringle was attacked last night," Lindal said, staring into the fire. "Everyone in the town heard their cries and woke."

"As did we," Lief whispered, remembering the distant screams he had heard in the darkness of the night.

"Many people in Ringle snatched up weapons and hurried to the camp," Lindal said. "But by the time we reached it, the guards were dead — dead and burning."

"Burning!" whispered Jasmine. She glanced at Lief, and a wave of heat swept over him.

It cannot be! he told himself. *No! It cannot . . .*

Barda wet his lips. "They must have been taken by surprise," he said with difficulty. "Attacked by someone they would never suspect. Treachery . . ."

Suddenly, he looked suspiciously at Lindal. "And how did you just happen to be in Ringle last night of all nights, Lindal of Broome?" he asked, his hand moving to the hilt of his sword.

Lindal lifted her chin. "I do not have to answer to you, you bumbling ox," she sneered. "Any more than you have to tell me why you are traveling inland instead of by the coast road, as planned."

Her lip curled. "Or why you chose to play the hero in the Forests of Silence while your men went on to Ringle, and their deaths," she added.

With a roar Barda sprang to his feet, drawing his sword, scattering the remains of his meal into the fire.

But Lindal was up just as quickly, a spear already in her hand.

Glowering, the two giants faced each other over the fire, their weapons gleaming, their bodies dyed scarlet by the light of the glowing coals.

"Barda!" thundered Lief. "Lindal! Stop!"

But neither Lindal nor Barda moved a muscle.

"You are fools, both of you," cried Jasmine in disgust. "You are shocked and grieved, so to relieve your feelings you turn on each other. Oh, very good!"

Lindal's eyes slid in her direction. The hand holding the spear tightened. For a terrifying moment Lief thought that Jasmine had spoken her mind once too often.

Then the hand relaxed, and the spear was lowered so it pointed to the ground.

"I was staying the night in Ringle because Ringle is on the way to the Os-Mine Hills," Lindal said, looking straight at Barda. "I had heard reports of a disturbance in the Hills. Screams and bursts of fire."

The Dragon hunting the Granous, Lief thought numbly. *Of course.*

"I have traveled the Hills many times," Lindal went on coldly. "I thought I would do my king a service by investigating the disturbance, so I could report when I met him in Broome. I am a loyal Deltoran — whatever others may think."

Barda put down his sword and bent his head.

"I beg pardon for doubting you," he muttered. "I just — cannot take this in. We thought *we* were the ones in danger. An enemy had been setting traps for us. That is why we entered the Forests. We never dreamed our escort would be attacked."

He shook his lowered head, his face grief-stricken. "Those guards were handpicked men — fine fighters, fine soldiers! How could they have been destroyed?"

"They had no chance," Lindal said grimly. "No chance without the Belt of Deltora to protect them."

The words stung Lief like a lash. His eyes blurred as Lindal dropped her spear and bent to the leather bag that lay beside her, pulling out a roll of what looked like stiff, brown parchment.

"It must have been a sudden, terrible attack," Lindal said, straightening slowly with the roll in her hand. "The whole camp was blackened, smoking, blasted by flame. The horses were running wild in the fields, mad with fear. The men — had been torn to pieces. The shreds of their bodies were in a heap, and the heap was burning."

Lief's throat tightened. He knew the truth now. His childish wish to be free had killed twelve brave men.

And Rolf, the Capricon.

You will be perfectly safe, Rolf, I promise.

His own words came back to haunt him. Had Rolf remembered them as he died — died, as long ago

the people of Capra had died? Torn, burning, screaming . . .

Lindal's mouth twisted. "It was a terrible sight,"
she said softly. "Even in the time of the Shadow Lord,
I saw nothing like it. I wish I could forget it."

Barda groaned softly.

"Somehow, one man had escaped the fire," said
Lindal, glancing at him. "A man with the Shadow
Lord's brand on his cheek."

"Brid," Jasmine murmured. "Brid . . ."

"He was terribly burned," Lindal said. "There
was a great wound in his chest, and his leg had been
torn off at the knee. But he was valiant. Still he managed to crawl to a tree and write — write a message in
his own blood."

She held out the stiff brown roll. "I peeled off the
bark with my knife. I thought it best that the people of
Ringle did not see it."

Lief took the bark from her hand and unrolled it.

Lief stared at the scrawled words in horror.

"It — it is impossible," he said haltingly. "Brid must have been seeing visions, because of loss of blood. Perhaps bandits . . ."

"No bandits could do what I saw," said Lindal. "And some of the people hurrying with me to the camp said they had seen a huge shadow in the sky, flying east. It looked like a dragon of old, they said."

She shrugged. "I told them they were dreaming — that there had been no dragons in Deltora for hundreds of years. Then I reached the place, and found the message on the tree. And now I do not know what to think."

"I do," muttered Barda. "I know very well what to think."

Lindal's face did not change, but she watched him closely.

Barda swung around to Lief, his fists clenched.

"Lindal of Broome may as well know the truth, Lief, for soon everyone will," he said bitterly. "We have roused something we cannot control. The golden dragon lied to you. It deceived you utterly, with its talk of borders and oaths. As soon as it had regained its strength, it came after us, hungry for blood."

Lief's heart was pounding. Lindal's words as she described what the people of Ringle had seen were still ringing in his ears.

. . . a huge shadow in the sky, flying east.

Why would the topaz dragon fly east? Why, its hunger satisfied, would it not return to its lair in the Os-Mine Hills?

He forced his stiff lips to move.

"I may indeed have roused something I cannot control, Barda," he said. "But I do not think it is the topaz dragon. I think . . . I fear . . . it is something worse."

15 - Fears and Visions

The next few days, trudging across the barren plain with Lindal, were among the worst Lief had ever spent.

That first night, he had told his companions of his fear. He had seen the lines deepen on their faces as they listened and understood. He had sat and talked with them for many hours, making decisions, forming plans.

At dawn the next day, Kree had set out for Del with a message for Doom. The companions knew that news of the tragedy at Ringle would spread quickly, and that Doom would soon hear of it. A description of Brid would alert him to the fact that the dead men were the royal escort, far from the coast road where they were supposed to be.

And unless he heard otherwise, he would certainly think that Lief, Barda, and Jasmine had shared the guards' fate.

Lief had written the note with a heavy heart, using a simple code that he and Doom had used several times before.

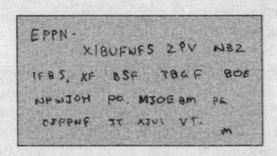

It was strange to be walking without Kree wheeling ahead of them. Jasmine was very quiet. She was concerned about Filli, who was bruised and listless, and Lief knew she also feared for Kree, because the skies were no longer safe.

Bitterly he regretted that his actions had brought them to this.

All the talk, all the planning, had not relieved his guilt, or his anger with himself.

Jasmine, Barda, and Lindal had not breathed a word of blame, but he knew he had failed them. As he had failed the guards, and Rolf, and all the people of the east, who now faced terror as well as famine.

Time and again, trudging over the rough, bare ground by day, lying beneath the canopy of stars by night, he remembered riding on the narrow path beside End Wood Gap, his fingers pressed to the great ruby.

He had tried to summon the ruby dragon. He had been quite sure that he had failed.

But what if he had not failed?

What if the ruby dragon had stirred indeed? What if it had woken in some dank hiding place nearby and lain still for a time, gathering strength?

What if it had remained hidden until Lief and the Belt were long gone into the Forests of Silence, and only then crawled into the light, its belly gnawed by the hunger of centuries?

Never had Lief considered, when he called to the ruby dragon, that it might not come to him at once, as the topaz dragon had.

Never had he dreamed that it might simply take to the skies with nothing on its mind except filling its belly.

But he feared there was no other way to explain what had happened in the camp near Ringle.

The topaz dragon had no grudge against the guards or Rolf — it had never even seen them. If it was just in search of food, surely it would have raided one of the villages closer to the Hills. And if it was seeking the Belt of Deltora, it would have followed Lief into the Forests of Silence.

It would have had no reason to attack the guards.

But the ruby dragon, ravenous after its long sleep, drawn to the camp by the scent of the Capricon, its ancient prey, would have had every reason.

Just as it would have had good reason to fly east, when its terrible feast was done — to fly east to Broome, where once stood Capra, its conquest of long ago.

Or to fly even farther, perhaps, to the place called Dragon's Nest.

✳

They reached the end of the plain and began climbing through a range of low hills. Very near them, to the north, the rugged mountains that marked the Shadowlands border rose dark and sinister against the sky.

Lief, Barda, and Jasmine knew from the map that on the other side of the hills lay that narrow, isolated part of Deltora that stretched like a bony finger into the wild eastern sea. They knew that when they reached the hills' highest point, they would look down on the coast, and the lonely city of Broome.

But even if they had not known, Lindal's behavior would have told them. She had begun to walk faster. Often she lifted her head and sniffed the air.

Lief knew that she was checking for the smell of fire. She was dreading what she might see when at last she looked down at her home.

She feared as he did, as Barda and Jasmine

feared also, that history might have repeated itself, and that nothing would be left by the sea but smoking ruins.

But when at last they peered down at the city of Broome, they saw at once that all was well.

The city was solid and untouched, the bright flags on its square white towers whipping in the crisp breeze.

Carts trundled along its roads. Fishing boats with red and yellow sails bobbed in its sparkling harbor.

"The dragon has not been here," Lindal said.

She turned to Lief, relief shining in her eyes.

"Do you see?" she said. "Every flag has been raised. Broome is preparing for your visit. But if we go quietly past, we will not be noticed. You are not expected so soon, and the guards will pay no attention to four dusty travelers."

Lief gazed down at the bright, welcoming city. Grimly he wondered how many flags would be flying if the people of Broome knew of the menace he had unleashed in their territory.

At least I do not have to face them now, he thought as Lindal began leading the way downward.

They had made their plan the night Lief confessed his fears of the ruby dragon and, throwing all caution aside, told Lindal of the quest to find the Sister of the East.

They had decided that if they found Broome safe, they would go straight on to Dragon's Nest, to face whatever was awaiting them there.

Lindal was to guide them. That had been decided, too — or, rather, Lindal had announced it, and refused to listen to any argument.

"Of course I must take you," she cried. "I have known the way to Dragon's Nest since my earliest years. It was forbidden to me then. My mother threatened me with a beating if ever I was to go near it. And so, of course, I went as near to it as I dared, whenever I could. As a child I was foolish and willful, and had no sense."

"And what has changed?" Barda demanded.

Lindal roared with laughter. "Why, now I am big enough to do as I please without fear of a beating," she said. "Unless you wish to fight me yourself, old bear?"

"No," Barda growled. "I might lose, and that would not be good for the pride of chief of the guards."

But he grinned as he said it. It had been clear to all that he would be very glad of Lindal's company.

Lief looked along the coast to the left of Broome's harbor, along the line of foaming white where waves crashed against the jagged rocks.

Gradually the mountains of the Shadowlands border closed in on the white line as if marching towards the sea. And at last, at Deltora's most eastern point, the rocks of coast and mountains met and mingled in a tumble of gray stone.

Somewhere in that grim confusion was the place called Dragon's Nest. There, Lief was sure now, they would find the ruby dragon.

The memory of Doran's hasty scrawl in the *Deltora Annals* was clear in his mind.

> I now know why the Enemy wanted the Dragons destroyed. He had a plan that the Dragons would not have tolerated.

Lief was sure that once its first, terrible hunger had been satisfied, the ruby dragon had sensed the intruder in its territory, and sped to Dragon's Nest to destroy it.

Perhaps even now it is doing our work for us, he thought, plodding doggedly after Lindal.

But the flicker of hope was small, and battered by the chill winds of fear. The ruby dragon was out of control. And it was only one.

Without the Belt to aid it, it might fail to destroy the evil thing hidden in Dragon's Nest. Then its rage would be terrible indeed. It would lash out at anything that crossed its path.

And soon it would be hungry again.

❋

The shadows were lengthening by the time they reached the bottom of the hills, and, as Lindal had promised, they slipped by Broome unnoticed.

When they were well past and the sun had begun to set, Lief turned to look back.

What he saw made him gasp. He stood, staring, unable to believe his eyes.

The city was bathed in pink light — and its whole shape had changed. It had become a dreaming, magical place of tall, delicate spires and shining glass domes.

Its sturdy outer walls had gone. In their place were groves of slender trees hung with glowing red globes that clinked softly together in the breeze making sweet, chiming music.

So beautiful . . .

His eyes filled with tears.

"Lief, what is the matter?" exclaimed Jasmine. She, too, spun around to look at the city, but clearly she could see nothing unusual.

"Ah — he can see Capra," said Lindal quietly. "The topaz in the Belt makes him sensitive, no doubt — and sunset is the dangerous time, they say."

She took Lief's arm and shook it.

"It is not real, Lief," she whispered. "It is a dream of something that is dead and gone. Turn away from it."

Lief did not move.

Lindal tugged his arm more roughly, almost pulling him off his feet, then began to walk briskly again, dragging him after her.

He stumbled at her heels, shaking his head as if waking from a dream.

"So beautiful . . ." he mumbled.

"Beautiful, but dangerous," Lindal said, striding on. "Keep walking! I should have warned you, but I had forgotten the old tales. Few ordinary mortals ever see Capra. No one from Broome has seen it in my lifetime."

She felt Lief dragging his feet and tightened her grip on his arm.

"Do not turn around again," she warned him. "You are fortunate you were not alone when you saw the illusion. There are tales of lone travelers who have died of thirst, so long did they stand with their eyes fixed on Capra. Once you have seen it, it captures your mind and holds you. Or so the old folk say."

"A ghost city!" muttered Barda, fascinated.

"Yes. They say that is why the last of the Capricons still haunt the mountains, instead of moving into Broome or building a new city of their own," Lindal said, keeping up her fast pace. "They watch for Capra at sunset. The old ones teach the young ones to love it, and to mourn what they have lost."

"But Capra was destroyed before the time of Adin!" Jasmine cried. "How long ago was that?"

Lindal shrugged. "If the Capricons would rather grieve over what is lost than live in the present, that is their own affair," she said carelessly. "They cannot be persuaded differently. The few that are left keep to themselves, and look down on everyone else."

"Rolf was not like that," Lief said, finding his voice. "He left the mountains and journeyed towards Del, to seek help for his people."

And so was killed by his worst nightmare.

The thought pierced him like a dart.

"Your friend would have found help in plenty if he had simply gone into Broome," said Lindal curtly. "He would also have learned that you were on your way there, and he had only to wait. But he would not enter Broome, oh, no!"

She shook her head, striding on, her eyes fixed on the horizon. "He would not lower himself to speak to ordinary mortals. Only the king himself was good enough to deserve the notice of a Capricon!"

"He had been brought up to think so," Lief murmured. "His ancestors — "

Lindal bared her teeth. "*My* ancestors were great warriors, who ate the brains of their slaughtered enemies," she said. "Do you suggest I do the same?"

"Lindal is perfectly right," snapped Jasmine.

"Rolf was cowardly, vain, and foolish. Why deny it, just because he is dead? I think — "

"I think we should stop arguing and light some torches," Barda put in calmly. "I can barely see my hand in front of my face, but there is something written on a stone ahead, and I suspect it is a warning."

16 ~ Dragon's Nest

The stone was very old, and looked unpleasantly like a tombstone. The very sight of it filled Lief with dread. He had to force himself to approach it, and lift his torch to read the words engraved upon it.

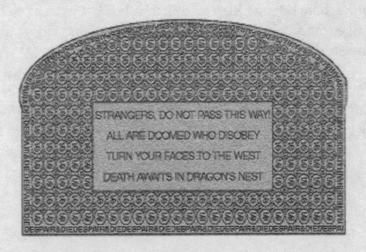

STRANGERS, DO NOT PASS THIS WAY!

ALL ARE DOOMED WHO DISOBEY

TURN YOUR FACES TO THE WEST

DEATH AWAITS IN DRAGON'S NEST

Jasmine shivered. "This stone gives me a bad feeling," she said. "Who made it?"

"No one knows," said Lindal. "It has always been here — and it has kept most people well away from Dragon's Nest."

"But not you," Barda said gruffly.

"Not me," Lindal admitted. "As I told you, I was a willful, disobedient child. Still, I hated to pass this stone. I always shut my eyes so I could not see it. I do not quite know why — or why I used to have nightmares about it afterwards. The verse is ominous, but . . ."

"It is not just the verse," Lief said slowly.

It had become extremely cold. Waves were crashing on the rocks, very near. He realized that without noticing it they had almost reached the tumble of rocks they had seen from the hills. A sickening trembling had begun deep within his body. His arm felt unbearably heavy as he held his torch flame closer to the stone.

"It is not just the verse," he repeated. "It is the carving in the background. Do you see? Those marks are the Sister signs, repeated endlessly. And the border . . ."

Barda leaned forward, peered at the border, then looked up, shaken. "Despair and die . . ." he muttered.

Filli whimpered beneath Jasmine's collar. She put up her hand to soothe him.

144

"The whole stone is a curse," she said softly. "It is an evil thing — full of hate."

"Come away from it," Lindal said abruptly, taking a step back.

Barda forced a grin, his white teeth gleaming in the darkness. "It seems you were braver as a child than you are now, Lindal!" he said.

"Only more foolish," Lindal retorted. "But still I never passed by the stone in darkness. The way to Dragon's Nest is fearful, even in daylight. At night — "

Lief backed away from the stone, gripping the Belt of Deltora with both hands. With relief he felt his mind begin to clear and the deep trembling to ease.

"We must stop in any case," he managed to say. "We need food and sleep. We will move on in the morning. Everything seems better in the light."

Lindal chose a camping spot well away from the evil stone. They lit a small fire for warmth and comfort. They ate, and at last they slept, keeping watch in turns.

But their sleep was far from peaceful. The sound of the crashing waves was cold and lonely. Dark, formless shadows haunted their dreams.

※

They set off at first light the following day. One by one they passed the standing stone, their eyes turned away from it, fixed on the churning sea.

Beyond the stone there was no path to follow —

only a wilderness of huge rocks piled one upon the other.

Lindal led the way, scrambling through the maze, more often crawling than walking upright. Lief, Barda, and Jasmine soon realized that without her they would have become hopelessly lost.

Kree had still not returned. No one spoke of it, but fear for him hung over them like a cloud.

On they went, and on. They could see nothing but cold stone, the looming mountains, and the sky. They could hear nothing but the booming of the waves, beating like a great drum.

There was no sign of life at all. Everything was cold and dead.

Their fingers grew numb and clumsy. A feeling of dread was growing within them, weighing them down.

Despair and die . . .

Lief shook his head, trying to rid himself of the memory of the message on the stone. But it clung in his mind like an evil tick, draining his strength, spreading its poison.

The mountains of the Shadowlands border grew larger, closer. The sound of the waves grew louder. They could feel the tingling of sea spray on their faces, and taste salt on their chilled lips, but still they could see nothing.

And then, at last, Lindal stopped at the foot of a great slab of rock that slanted upward.

She waited until they caught up with her, then crawled with them to the top of the slab.

"There," she said in a low voice.

Straight ahead of them the stones fell away into a vast, bowl-shaped hollow squeezed between the mountains and the sea. The hollow was so deep that from where the companions lay, clutching the edge of the slanting rock, they could not see the bottom.

The mountains brooded over the hollow, glowering and secret. Waves crashed against its far edge, spattering the rocks with foam.

Lief guessed that at high tide the hollow was flooded with swirling water, for the stones that formed its sides were rounded and polished smooth, and strands of parched seaweed trailed over them like long, tangled hair.

Dragon's Nest . . .

Lief did not need to look at the emerald in the Belt of Deltora. He knew it would be as gray as the rock on which he lay. He could feel the evil crawling about him like a clammy mist, raising the hair on his arms and the back of his neck.

His mind swirled with shadows. His body was covered with freezing sweat, and the terrible, deep trembling had begun again.

Feebly he felt for the Belt, willing its magic to work for him as it had done so often before.

The topaz to clear his mind. The amethyst to soothe and calm. The diamond for strength . . .

"This was my lookout. I never went closer to the Nest than this," Lindal shouted over the sound of the pounding waves. "I was reckless as a child, but not quite mad."

She hunched her shoulders. "Ah — I had almost forgotten this feeling! It is as if some vile, invisible vapor rises from that hollow. It makes my skin crawl."

"It is the Sister of the East," Lief murmured through stiff lips. "The dragon has not been here — or has not been able to destroy it."

A great wave thundered onto the rocks with such force that the spray flew high into the air, raining down into the hollow, and spattering the companions with icy drops.

Gasping, they half slid, half clambered back down to the foot of the slanting rock.

"The tide is rising," Lindal said, shaking water from her painted head like a dog. "It took longer to get here than I remembered. We must move quickly — before the Nest begins to flood. Otherwise we will have to wait in this accursed place for hours until the tide turns again."

Together they moved forward. The sound of the waves was deafening. The cruel wind whistled around them, and every now and again they were sprayed with freezing foam.

By the time they reached the hollow they were crawling on their bellies, shivering and breathless.

They hauled themselves to the very edge. And as

they looked down, they all caught their breath in shock.

Whatever they had expected to see, it was not this.

The vast, stony bowl of the Nest was completely empty, except for a small, piteous figure lying huddled in the center.

Lief stared at the dark, curly head, the slender arms, the sprawled, furred legs tipped with delicate hoofs.

"Rolf!" he whispered. "It is Rolf! The dragon must have carried him off — brought him here. But why?"

"Any creature finds it useful to have a little of its favorite food put aside for later," Lindal pointed out, gazing down at the Capricon with interest.

At that moment, Rolf's crumpled body moved feebly.

"He is still alive," breathed Jasmine.

Lief's stomach knotted.

"Do not call to him! Do not make a sound!" Barda warned sharply, his eyes scanning the looming mountains. "The beast must be around somewhere. We do not want to alert it."

Impulsively Lief moved to hurl himself down the sloping sides of the Nest. Barda caught him and held him back.

"No, Lief!" Barda whispered. "Think! Once we are down there, we will be helpless if the dragon attacks. And I am not sure that Lindal is right. To me, the Capricon looks unpleasantly like bait."

"*Bait?*" hissed Lief. "Bait for what?"

Barda shrugged. "Possibly for other Capricons who roam the mountains. But I suspect — I fear — bait for us."

"Are you mad?" Lief struggled to tear himself free. "What does the ruby dragon know of us?"

"Have you forgotten the enemy who tricked us into going to End Wood Gap?" Barda demanded, tightening his grip. "What did that enemy do after we went into the Forests of Silence?"

Lief grew still. His mind was whirling.

"What if when the ruby dragon arose, our enemy's face was the first thing it saw, and our enemy's voice was the first sound it heard?" Barda demanded. "What if they formed some sort of alliance? To trap us, kill us, and defend the Sister of the East?"

Lief wet his lips. "That is impossible," he whispered.

"It does not seem likely," Lindal agreed. "From what the old folk say, dragons do not form alliances — even with one another. And surely your enemy hoped you would die in End Wood? As you nearly did, in fact."

"He might have hoped for it, but he would not have depended upon it," said Barda. "The Shadow Lord does not tolerate mistakes by his servants."

Lief shook his head stubbornly.

"The dragon would not harm me," he said. "Not while I wear the Belt of Deltora. And it would never agree to defend the Sister. No dragon would tolerate such a thing in its territory. Doran said — "

"Forget what Doran said!" Barda broke in. "Who knows what might have happened to the body and brain of a beast that has slept for centuries?"

He clenched his fists. "You cannot argue with the proof, Lief! The dragon has been here, but it has made no attempt to find the Sister and destroy it. The Nest has not been disturbed. Not a stone is out of place."

A giant wave smashed against the rocks beyond the Nest. Icy spray rained down. Far below them, the Capricon writhed and wailed.

"You are all wasting time," Jasmine snapped. "This argument is pointless! We are here to destroy the Sister of the East. We know that it is somewhere in Dragon's Nest — somewhere down there, hidden under the stones. So we must go into the Nest and dig for it. It is all very simple."

"Simple!" Barda growled. "With a dragon lurking and Rolf moaning and squirming around our feet?"

"Oh, we will have to get Rolf out first, I suppose," Jasmine said impatiently. "Otherwise he will get in our way."

"Lief will have to go down for him," said Lindal,

peering down at the wailing Capricon. "It would be too much to hope that he would cooperate with anyone else, even to save his own life."

Jasmine nodded and turned to Lief, pulling the coil of rope she carried from her belt.

"Barda must lower you down, Lief," she said. "The stones on the sides of the Nest look far too loose to support you. Take my rope for Rolf. Then Barda and Lindal can pull you both up together."

Lindal grinned broadly. "Why, how this little mouse is ordering us about, old bear!" she jeered, digging Barda in the ribs. "Are you going to take that?"

"It seems I am," Barda muttered as Lief began tying his own rope around his waist. "I fear I have no choice."

17 ~ Fire and Water

As Jasmine had feared, there were no safe footholds on the sloping sides of the Nest. The stones slid downward the moment they were touched, setting Lief swinging at the end of the rope like a puppet. And the lower he dropped, the colder it grew, and the more he was gripped by dread.

It is the Sister, he told himself, struggling to keep his mind clear. But his teeth had begun to chatter and his heart was pounding in his chest as though it would burst.

He landed awkwardly on the floor of the Nest, sinking almost to his knees in the bed of smooth stones. Stones slipped beneath his feet, and dried weed tangled around his ankles as he stumbled towards Rolf, the end of Jasmine's rope clutched in his hand.

The stones are deep, he thought numbly. *Very, very*

deep. *How far down is the Sister of the East? How long will it take to find it? It may not even be below the floor of the Nest. It may be in one of the sides. What then?*

Waves of sickness threatened to engulf him. Every step was an effort. He realized that he had begun to stagger.

This place will defeat us, he thought suddenly. *Its evil is too strong. No one could dig in these stones for more than a few minutes at a time. We are going to fail.*

Fighting despair, he reached Rolf's crumpled body and knelt down beside him.

"Rolf!" he croaked, the word sticking in his throat.

With a choking cry the Capricon sat up. He snatched at Lief and clung to him, his huge violet eyes swimming with terrified tears.

"Oh, why did you abandon me?" he moaned. "The guards did not protect me! You said they would protect me, but they did not! Oh, the screams — the blood — the fire! Never will I forget it!"

"I know, Rolf," Lief muttered. "Be still now."

"The dragon seized me . . . carried me — " Suddenly, Rolf broke off and looked around in bewilderment. "But where are your friends?" he squeaked. "Did they not come with you?"

"They are waiting at the top," said Lief briefly. With difficulty he freed his arms and began looping Jasmine's rope around Rolf's waist.

"Oh!" Rolf covered his face with his hands and

rocked from side to side. "Oh, soon the dragon will return! We must get away!"

"Stay still then!" begged Lief. He pulled at the rope to make sure it was secure, then hauled Rolf to his feet and, with the last of his strength, half carried him to the side of the Nest.

Jasmine was standing up above, keeping watch. Barda and Lindal were kneeling, peering over the edge of the Nest, the ropes gripped ready in their hands.

Lief signaled to them and at once they began to pull the ropes up, hand over hand.

Rolf looked up as the rope tightened around his waist and his feet left the floor of the Nest. When he saw Lindal's grim face and straining arms above him, he shrieked.

"Be quiet!" Lief whispered.

"But the woman of Broome is lifting me!" cried Rolf in horror. "How could you let *her* lift me? She and her kind are demons who dance on the bones of Capra! She is not worthy to — "

"Shut your mouth, Rolf!" hissed Lief.

But Lindal had heard. "I am happy to drop you if you wish, Capricon," she called.

Rolf whimpered and pressed his lips together. He clung to the rope, a dead weight, as slowly he and Lief were dragged upward over the loose and sliding stones.

But the moment he reached the top, he scrambled away from Lindal, avoiding her hand.

"Do not touch me, foul woman of Broome!" he gabbled, tearing the rope from his waist and casting it aside as though it were poisoned. "Keep away from me!"

"It would be a pleasure," said Lindal scornfully.

Barda gripped the hilt of his sword "How do you dare to insult Lindal, who has risked her life to save you?" he growled, looking at Rolf with contempt.

Eyeing the sword warily, Rolf crawled to his feet.

"My king," he cried in a trembling voice. "Your man is menacing me!"

But Lief, still slumped on the ground where Barda had left him, knew he could not interfere, even if he wanted to. He felt sick and desperately weak, as though stricken with a grave illness. He could only wonder how Rolf could move.

Barda took a threatening step towards the cowering Capricon.

"Lindal has more strength in her little finger than you have in your whole body," he growled. "She has a better brain than you will ever possess, and a bigger heart than a hundred of you put together!"

"Why, thank you, Barda," murmured Lindal, raising her eyebrows. "Though, now I come to think of it, it is not so great a compliment."

Barda ignored her. "Get out of my sight!" he spat at Rolf. "Go and hide your miserable self from the dragon, and trouble us no more!"

With a gulp and a last, beseeching glance at Lief, Rolf scuttled away. Soon he had disappeared among the giant stones.

"Good riddance," said Jasmine calmly. "Now we can get down to work. How should we begin?"

Feeling her eyes upon him, Lief made an effort to sit up. A wave of dizziness overcame him, and he fell back with a groan.

He heard Barda and Jasmine exclaim, and felt them kneel beside him. He tried to focus on their anxious faces, looming above him amid a spinning haze.

"I — I do not know where to begin," he mumbled. "I do not know what to do. The Belt does not help me. In the Nest, there is evil everywhere. It batters you from all sides. It is . . ."

Despair and die.

Another giant wave smashed on the rocks. Freezing water rained down on them and ran in streams into the Nest.

"We have to get him away from here," Lief heard Barda mutter.

"No!" Lief managed to say. "The feeling is passing. Just give me a moment to — "

"BEWARE!"

Lindal's cry rose high and urgent over the sound of the waves. A freezing gale suddenly pounded down upon the rocks. A dark shadow swept overhead, blocking the sun.

Jasmine and Barda cried out, sprang to their feet.

And as they moved, Lief saw a horror above him — a vast, bloated thing of glittering scarlet.

The beast's spiked wings sliced through the air like knives. The stunted mass of lumps and spines that was its tail twisted and thrashed. Its tiny red eyes, almost hidden amid puffy folds of scaly skin, were the mad eyes of a killer.

Who knows what might have happened to the body and brain of a beast that has slept for centuries?

Barda's words roared in Lief's mind.

Desperately he struggled to get to his feet, fighting the dizziness, the weakness. Desperately he fumbled for his sword.

Curved black talons, impossibly long, struck viciously downward. Lief rolled, and a claw missed him by a hair, scraping on the rock.

The creature roared in fury — a harsh, high sound like shattering glass. Fire belched from its gaping jaws. Boiling red slime dripped from its fangs and fell, sizzling, onto the streaming rocks. Steam billowed upward.

Lost in the steam, blind and helpless, Lief gripped the Belt of Deltora.

He fixed his mind upon the great ruby. With all his strength he willed the dragon to feel the power of the great gem, to hear him and understand.

But the beast bellowed in rage and madness and came for him again, a monstrous glistening fury, red as blood.

Lief felt Jasmine and Barda seize his arms and haul him back. He heard the razor-sharp claws scrape the rock again, felt the hot blast of fire on his face.

A wave thundered onto the tall rocks behind them. Cold spray drenched them, instantly turning to steam in the monster's fire.

Barda was bellowing over the sound of the waves.

". . . get as close to the water as we can!" Barda was shouting. "Our only chance . . ."

But the dragon was above them, striking at them, sending them sprawling on the greasy stone, rolling and scrabbling away from its clawing feet, its bursts of fire.

And then, through the swirling veil of steam, Lief saw the tall figure of Lindal standing her ground, her spear arm raised.

"Lindal!" Barda bellowed, scrambling to his feet. "Get down!"

A spear flew through the air. It struck the dragon's thrashing tail, bounced away, and clattered uselessly to the ground.

Lindal did not falter. Another spear was already in her hand. She hurled it, and this time it reached its mark — its point piercing the softer, paler flesh of the monster's belly.

The monster screeched, clawed the waving spear from its body, and wheeled to face its attacker.

They all saw Lindal's teeth flash in a savage grin of triumph. "Now! Go!" she shouted.

Barda hesitated.

"Barda!" shrieked Jasmine, pulling at his arm.

"Do not make this all for nothing, you bumbling ox!" roared Lindal, reaching for her last spear. "Get to the water!"

And with a groan Barda obeyed her. He turned his back on her, seized Lief with his free arm, and leaped for the tall rocks where the sea pounded upon the land, where spray now rained down unceasingly, and water ran in streams.

They squeezed into a gap between the rocks and turned, in terror, just in time to see Lindal fall — fall, crumpled and bleeding, beneath the monster's beating wing.

The beast's ghastly head turned on its swollen neck. It glared at its fallen enemy. It roared, and a plume of fire belched downward.

Lindal's clothes burst into flames. The puddles on the stones around her hissed and steamed.

Lief and Jasmine cried out in grief and horror. But Barda stood rigid and silent as the rock.

A giant wave thundered behind them, and this time the water frothed over them in a flood, streaming over the smooth stones, running down into Dragon's Nest.

The beast snarled. It shook its head as if to clear its eyes. And then, suddenly, its neck twisted again —

twisted away from Lindal. Suddenly, it was looking up — up into the swirling steam above its head.

It gave a broken cry, its crooked mouth gaping, its forked tongue darting. Its leathery wings began to flap wildly. Its ungainly body jerked, turning this way and that as if in panic. Its spiked, stubby tail thrashed on the steaming rock.

Then abruptly the billowing steam was swept away — swept away as if by a great wind. And Lief's heart leaped as he saw, plunging down from the sky, a vast, glittering creature red as the setting sun, with eyes like glowing coals, wings like scarlet sails, and a tail sleek and slender as a stream of fire.

"Another dragon!" Jasmine gasped. "Another ruby dragon!"

But Lief was looking down at the Belt of Deltora, at the glowing, scarlet star that the great ruby had become, and was wondering how ever he could have been deceived.

"No," he shouted. "Not another ruby dragon. *The* ruby dragon. The true ruby dragon has risen at last."

18 - Fight to the Death

Snarling, the monster on the ground rose to defend itself. It clawed the air, and fire spurted from his jaws. But then its enemy was upon it, and in moments the battle was over.

Indeed, it was no battle at all, for the rage-filled beast that had answered Lief's desperate call had a dragon's heart, mind, and will, and the nightmare copy on the ground did not.

The copy could tear frail humans apart, and its fire could burn their flesh to blackened cinders, but it was no match for the most ancient and mysterious of Deltora's beasts.

In seconds it was on its back, its throat torn and bleeding, its body heaving as its life drained away.

The ruby dragon raised its head, spread its wings, and roared its savage triumph as waves thundered on the rocks and spray flew upward to fall like rain.

It licked its lips, as if tasting the salt. Its great head turned towards the sea.

And as the echo of its roar still growled like thunder in the Mountains, it launched itself into the air and was gone.

Lief, Barda, and Jasmine crawled shakily out of hiding. They were drenched, and very cold. Shivering, they turned towards the crashing waves and looked up.

The ruby dragon was a vivid splash of scarlet against the blue sky. Water streamed from its scales. In its mouth was the flashing silver of a wriggling fish. The fish disappeared. The dragon wheeled and dived again.

"It will be back," Barda muttered. He began to move across the stones, towards the place where Lindal fell.

The scarlet beast lay across their path. Its scales had darkened to the color of dried blood, but all of them could see that it still lived.

As they cautiously approached it, its tiny eyes opened and fixed them with a look of dull hatred.

"Keep back," Jasmine muttered. "It would strike at us, even now, if it could."

The beast hissed, as if with loathing, and suddenly the bulbous folds of its misshapen body began to heave and roll like the waves on the sea, the scales shimmering like dark water.

The companions jumped back, staring in disbelief as the rippling mound of flesh collapsed in on itself and melted away.

Then it had gone, and all that was left lying on the stones was the sprawled, torn body of Rolf the Capricon.

"Rolf!" Lief whispered. And, all at once, a long line of things that had puzzled him made perfect sense.

Rolf's reckless exposure of him to the Granous. The dimming of the ruby when no enemy could be seen. The lightening of his heart as the guards, with Rolf, moved away. The guard troop, taken by surprise despite the night watch. The sparing of the horses. Rolf's lack of surprise on seeing that Lindal was with them. Rolf's strength after being in the Nest . . .

And most of all, the false dragon, ugly as a nightmare in a fevered brain.

Rolf's pale lips stretched into a malicious smile.

"You fools!" he said. "How easily I deceived you! A finger was a small price to pay for your trust. The sacrifice of my pride was not."

His head rolled from side to side. "Do you think I did not know how you despised me?" he hissed. "Me! — the one who could have transformed and torn you limb from limb in a moment — if it had not been for that accursed Belt."

He paused, panting, licking his foam-flecked lips.

"I knew I had to wait — wait until you reached the home of the Sister, the heart of my power, where even the Belt could not save you. So I watched and stayed my hand, even when the loathsome woman of Broome joined you and I longed to attack."

His hands twitched, clutching at the air. His hatred was almost visible. It was as if it oozed from the pores of his skin, and hung about him like a poisonous cloud.

"I had hoped you would all come into the pit, but you cheated me and did not," he rasped. "So again I waited, until you were all together once more, for I had sworn a mighty oath that not one of you would escape my wrath, as you escaped it at End Wood Gap."

He smiled crookedly, "Not for a moment did you suspect me," he breathed. "I was too clever for you."

"You do not look so clever now," snarled Barda, staring down at him.

Rolf sneered. "Your evil beast has been the death of me, but there are others — other servants of the Master — who lie in wait for you. This is your last battle, scum of the land. And it is a battle you will never win."

"What did the Shadow Lord promise you, that you would betray your king?" asked Lief dully.

"You are not my king, Lief of Del," Rolf spat.

"What did you know of me, before I threw myself in your way in the Os-Mine Hills? What did you know of Rolf, eldest son of the clan Dowyn, heir to the lordship of Capra?"

"I knew nothing," Lief said quietly. "But how could I have known, Rolf? You kept yourself secret and apart, even from the people of Broome."

"Do not argue with him, Lief," murmured Jasmine. "Truth does not matter to him. His mind feeds on pride and anger, nothing more."

"You cared nothing for me, king," Rolf said. "But the Master knew me, and knew my worth. The Master's voice came to me one night at sunset, as I huddled alone in the Mountains, looking down at Capra. The Master understood my greatness. He gave me precious gifts, in return for my service. And much more will follow . . . so much more . . ."

His breath was coming in shallow gasps now. His beautiful violet eyes were glazed.

"I serve the Master," he whispered. "For the Master, I will protect the Sister of the East. And in return he has made me a great sorcerer. I can do things of which my ancestors never dreamed. I can change shape. I can fly through the air. I can tear and burn my enemies, and hear them scream, as they deserve."

Barda cursed under his breath. His fists were clenched. But he said nothing aloud and made no move.

"When the Master triumphs, I will be the ruler of the East, as is my birthright," Rolf rasped. "Capra will rise again, and the vile strangers in my land will be dust and ashes beneath my feet."

Again he smiled. And then his gaze grew fixed, and the restless twitching of his hands stilled. He was dead.

The companions turned away, sickened.

A wave pounded on the rocks. Spray pelted down. Water foamed between the stones.

And in the brief quiet before another wave struck, they all distinctly heard a low groan.

They scrambled towards the sound.

Lindal had rolled into a deep cleft between two rocks. The left side of her face bore the raised scarlet mark of the dragon's pounding wing. Her clothes were blackened and her left arm was blistered. Her eyes were glazed and blinking. She was drenched to the skin.

But she was alive!

"Help me out of this accursed hole," she slurred, holding up her uninjured arm. "Every time a wave breaks, water flows over me like a stream. I am freezing!"

"Stop complaining," shouted Barda, joyfully hauling her upright. "The last we saw of you, you were burning like a torch! The wave must have put the fire out."

Lindal stood swaying and shivering, looking around her blankly. Plainly she could not understand what had happened.

She saw Rolf's body lying on the stones and frowned in puzzlement. Then she looked up and her face twisted in alarm.

"The dragon is returning!" she shouted. "It is coming straight for us!"

And the dragon was coming, indeed — flying back from the sea, its scarlet body wet and gleaming, brilliant against the sky.

Filli began chattering frantically. He had had quite enough of dragons.

Lindal felt for her spears, remembered they were gone, and lurched forward, her eyes desperately searching the ground.

"My spears!" she mumbled. "I must find — "

Barda took her arm and gently drew her back. "Be still, Lindal," he said. "We will explain everything later. Just be still now, and wait."

They backed against the nearest rock. There was nowhere else to go.

A huge shadow swept over them. They bent beneath the wind of mighty wings. And then the wind abruptly ceased and they looked up.

The dragon had landed at the edge of the Nest. It was watching them calmly.

Speak to it, Lief told himself. *It is waiting.*

But his mouth was dry, and he felt as though his

back had become part of the rock. He summoned up his courage and forced himself to step forward.

The ruby dragon looked down at him and seemed to smile.

"So!" it said, its voice soft and whispering. "So you have come, king of Deltora, wearing the great ruby of my territory. It is just as Doran promised."

"Yes," Lief said. "I searched for you, and at last I found you."

"Or *I* found *you*," said the dragon. Its eyes flashed and its forked tail twitched.

"There is evil here," it said. "Evil and poison. You allowed an intruder to enter my land while I slept."

Lief felt a chill of fear, but forced himself to hold the dragon's blood-red gaze.

"Not I," he said. "It happened long, long ago. Can you destroy the evil? As you have destroyed its guardian?"

He glanced at the limp form of Rolf, lying on the stones.

"We will see," said the ruby dragon. "Come closer. You alone."

Lief did as he was bid, though his knees were trembling so that he could hardly stand.

"And closer still," the dragon said.

Lief moved so close that if he had stretched out his hand he could have touched the glittering red scales of the beast's neck. The scent of the dragon filled his nose. It was like the smell of hot metal mixed with burning leaves.

The ruby on the Belt of Deltora blazed like fire.

The dragon spread its wings and closed its eyes.

For a long moment it seemed to bask in the ruby's radiance. And when its eyes opened once more, it seemed to Lief that they were deeper and darker than they had been before.

"Now," the dragon said.

Its wings still spread, it plunged into the hollow called Dragon's Nest. With its mighty claws it began to rake away the stones in the center, scooping them out by the hundreds, by the thousands, flinging them up and away.

19 – The Sister of the East

Stones pelted the companions like giant hail. Covering their heads with their arms, they stumbled away from the edge of the Nest.

From a safe distance they stood and watched in awe as stones showered from the hollow to pile in great drifts around its rim. But gradually their excitement died, and a feeling of foreboding took its place.

As the dragon dug deeper into the pit, as the heaps of stones grew larger, the air was becoming thicker and harder to breathe. The light was dimming. And a strange, low ringing sound was growing louder.

Giant waves pounded on the shore, now sometimes foaming over the tops of the tall rocks and streaming down like a waterfall to run in rivulets between the stones.

But even the waves could not drown out the terrible song of the Sister of the East floating up from the hollow.

It was a song of barren despair, of ruin and misery, of dullness and death. One low note, haunting, penetrating, relentless.

And worst of all, strangely familiar.

Filli was whimpering beneath Jasmine's collar. Jasmine herself was hunched and frowning as if in pain. Lindal sat slumped on the stones, her head bowed, her hands pressed to her ears.

"I did not know," Barda murmured. Lief glanced at him. The big man's face was gleaming with sweat.

"I have been hearing this sound all my life," Barda muttered, his lips scarcely moving. "Not like this. Not so that I was aware of it. But now I realize that faintly it has always been there, like the sun on my face, or the air I breathe. I did not even think of it as sound. I thought it was the sound of silence."

"Yes," said Lief.

And then they both realized that the stones had stopped falling, and they could hear no movement inside the hollow.

"Where are you? Come to me!"

Lief did not know if the dragon had called in his mind or aloud.

It does not matter, he told himself slowly. *All that matters is that I must go.*

He forced himself to move forward, pushing

through the dull, thick air, scrambling up a towering heap of stones. He crawled to the very edge of the heap, and peered down into Dragon's Nest.

The broad, flat surface of the Nest had become a yawning pit at the base of a vast, stony funnel.

The dragon had dug down to the bare rock. Now it crouched on the rock, in the center of the pit, staring at the thing it had uncovered.

The thing was like a glowing, pulsating egg. It was a poisonous, flaring yellow, so bright that it seemed to hurt the eyes.

Its low, continuous song drilled into Lief's ears. And from it radiated evil so intense that his throat closed and his skin burned.

"Come to me, or I am lost."

The dragon's voice was very faint. Lief saw with terror that the rich scarlet of its scales was slowly dimming.

Without hesitation, without a thought, not even hearing Barda's shout of alarm, he flung himself over the edge.

Tumbling and gasping, he slid down through the piled stones, down into the pit where the dragon crouched.

He landed heavily near the beast's hind feet. A mass of stones came with him, beating on the dragon's folded wings, half covering its tail.

The dragon did not speak, did not move. There

was not a quiver of its skin or a twitch of a claw. Its great body was utterly motionless.

Lief tried to stand, and found he could not. The sinister song of the Sister of the East filled his ears and his mind. Its evil power battered him, beat him to the ground.

He could not stand. He could not walk. But the dragon lay rigid, fading as he watched. And the Sister of the East sang on, spreading its terror and its poison.

Lief began to crawl, being careful not to touch the dragon's body as he passed it.

His breath coming in sobbing gasps, he pushed himself towards the poisonous yellow thing that radiated horror and despair. He knew only that the thing must be destroyed — that if it could not be destroyed, all was lost.

But moment by moment, his strength was draining away. His arms and legs were trembling as if he was in the grip of a terrible fever, yet he was chilled to the bone. He feared that soon he would be unable to move at all.

Hardly knowing what he did, he pressed his hands to the great ruby in the Belt of Deltora.

Warmth stole through his fingers, rushed into his arms. And he became aware of a new sound mingling with the low song of the Sister.

It was a slow, heavy thumping sound, like the beating of a great drum. And slowly Lief realized that it was the dragon's heart.

The Belt . . . we are linked by the power of the Belt, he thought dimly.

Words flashed into his mind. Doran's words:

The king, wearing the Belt of Deltora, is Deltora's only salvation now.

Following an impulse he did not understand, but did not question, Lief lifted one hand from the Belt and placed it on the dragon's cool, dry skin.

Instantly his fingers tingled, and his own heart swelled in his chest as he felt power surge through him, rush through his body like a raging torrent from the great ruby to the beast.

The dragon stirred. The dull scales beneath Lief's hand brightened, deepened to rich scarlet. And Lief saw with wonder the patch of color spread from beneath his hand, spread surely and rapidly until the whole mighty body was glowing like the ruby itself.

The dragon raised its head. Its red eyes flashed. Its heartbeats crashed like thunder.

And still the power of the ruby streamed through Lief, and he could not have lifted his hand from the glowing scales even if he had wanted to.

He could not move or speak, but he knew it did not matter.

He was doing all he had to do. He was the link. He was the connection between the dragon and the ruby, the ancient talisman dug from deep within the dragon's earth.

The dragon fixed its red eyes on the pulsating

yellow egg before it. It roared, and a narrow jet of flame gushed from its mouth, wrapping the egg in fire.

Again the dragon roared, and again. Bathed in fire, the egg glowed red, then white. White-hot, it shimmered, burning like an evil star.

There was a sharp cracking sound as its surface split. Its low song rose to a shriek. For a long moment, it seemed that time stood still.

Then the dragon hissed like a giant snake. And beneath a fresh blast of heat so intense that Lief felt in terror that his own flesh must melt, the Sister of the East flashed with white flame, then simply withered and fell into dust.

Lief closed his burning eyes. As if suddenly released, his hand slipped from the dragon's side. He lay still, facedown on the rock, his mind empty of thought, aware of nothing but the crashing of the waves above and, beside him, the slow, steady beating of the dragon's heart.

✳

When Lief opened his eyes again, he found that he was no longer in the hollow with the ruby dragon. Or even at the edge of Dragon's Nest.

He could hear the waves, but they were some distance away. He was lying on a sleeping blanket, in front of a brightly burning fire.

On the other side of the fire, Barda, Jasmine, and Lindal were murmuring together. Firelight flickered on their faces, but their bodies were shadowy and behind them the light was dim and strangely stained with pink.

At first Lief feared that his sight had been damaged by the heat of the dragon's fire. Then he looked up.

The first thing he saw was Kree, perched on the tip of a jagged rock. Kree had returned at last!

Relief washed over him like cool water. Then he realized that Kree was silhouetted against a sky that was a riot of red and orange streaks, and he sighed with gratitude.

There was nothing wrong with his sight. The sun was going down!

Gingerly he sat up, feeling bruised all over.

"You have certainly taken your time to wake," Jasmine said. "We brought you out of that pit and carried you away from the spray hours ago!" Her voice was just as usual, but her face shone with relief.

"The dragon — " Lief broke off, wincing. His throat felt raw and scorched. He took the flask Jasmine passed to him, and drank gratefully.

"The dragon is at sea, hunting for more fish," said Barda, putting aside the little locked box he had been playing with. "I doubt we will see it again before morning."

"And I am glad of that," Jasmine said. "The beast makes me nervous. It seems to like the look of my hair even more than the other dragon did."

Lindal laughed, smoothing her smooth skull.

"It likes mine not at all!" she crowed. "Because it cannot see it! Which is exactly why it is a tradition for the women of my people to shave their heads clean."

Then her face sobered. "In the old days there were many scarlet dragons in the east. I have heard dread tales of them from the cradle. Now one, at least, has returned."

"Without it, the Sister of the East could not have been destroyed," Lief reminded her.

Lindal nodded. "I know," she said ruefully. "And I know that because the Sister has gone, the fields of the east will be fruitful again, and the fisher-folk will no longer come to shore with empty nets three days out of five. It is a cause for great rejoicing."

She sighed. "But still, it has come at a price. The dragon respects you, Lief, for you wear the Belt of Deltora. But I fear what may happen to the people of Broome when you move on. The mountains of the north are very far from — "

Jasmine gave an exclamation of annoyance, and Barda dug Lindal in the ribs. She clapped her hand over her mouth.

Lief's heart lurched. "The mountains of the north?" he exclaimed. "What — ?"

Avoiding his eyes, Barda picked up the little box and began turning it over in his hands again.

"No!" rasped Lief. "You must tell me! What do you know that I do not?"

"We had intended to wait until you were stronger before we told you," Jasmine murmured. "We wanted you to rest, just for tonight, and not to think about — "

"Not to think about what?" Lief roared, then groaned and grasped his aching throat.

Jasmine glanced at Barda. He shrugged reluctantly.

"While you slept, we buried Rolf, as is proper," he said. "But before that . . ."

"Before that, I searched the body," Jasmine said calmly, taking a yellowed, folded paper from one of her many pockets. "Which is *not* proper, according to Barda. But stitched into the hem of the Capricon's cloak, I found this."

She handed the paper to Lief. Eagerly he unfolded it. As he had hoped, it was the second part of Doran's map.

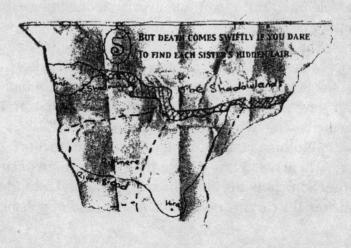

Jasmine leaned over to tap a finger on the Sister symbol. "There," she said. "That is why we will be going to the mountains of the north."

"Shadowgate," Lief muttered, reading the name beside the symbol. "I have never heard of it, or seen it on a map before!"

"Nor I," said Barda grimly, frowning at the box in his hands. "It does not sound an appealing place."

"Neither did Dragon's Nest," said Jasmine. "But at Dragon's Nest we made a lie of the verse printed here. We not only found the first Sister, but we destroyed it. And we survived! *That* is what we should be thinking of tonight, Lief."

She took the map fragment from Lief and put it away once more. "Tonight, we must rest and be glad," she said firmly. "What is the point of worrying about the future? It will come soon enough."

"Indeed!" Lindal agreed heartily. "This is a time to celebrate, not moan and worry about things that cannot be changed."

She sprang to her feet. "Let us go to Broome at once!" she cried. "We will take them by surprise, but all the better! I hate speeches and parades. Hot baths, fish stew, good ale, loud music, and friends to clap us on the back — what more could anyone ask?"

"Nothing at all," said Barda with satisfaction.

There was a tiny click and he gave a shout of surprise. Somehow his blunt fingers had found a hidden catch in the carving of the box. A small rod of polished wood now protruded from the cube, very near to the top.

He pulled eagerly at the box's lid, but it remained firmly closed. He looked up in comical dismay.

"There is more than one lock!" he exclaimed. "Curse this foolish toy!"

Lindal laughed uproariously. "Throw it away, old bear!" she cried. "You will never solve the puzzle."

"I will," Barda grunted, shoving the box back into his pocket. "I will solve it, if it is the last thing I ever do."

Cold fingers seemed to run down Lief's spine. He shivered, and wondered why.

I am cold, he told himself. *I am cold and tired, that is all.*

"Lief!" shouted Jasmine, jumping up and kicking at the fire to put it out. "Lief, are you ready?"

Her face was turned to him, full of love and laughter. Barda and Lindal towered behind her, scuffling with one another like children.

Lief's heart warmed.

What is the point of worrying about the future? It will come soon enough.

"Yes," he said, grinning and climbing to his feet. "Lead on! I am ready."